"Quit tortur...
woman!" h...

He clasped her slen...
brushed each toe with quick, loving kisses. Gail murmured, "Tyler Peabody, I love you. Oh, how I love
you. I cannot count the ways!"

"Try!" Tyler whispered.

Gail smiled. "I love you because you're suave and
debonair."

"More!" Tyler murmured, kissing the palms of her
hands.

"And I love you because of your worldly charm and
brilliance."

"More!" His lips circled her navel slowly, sensuously.

"And I love you because you're the best lover I've
ever known."

"Let's keep it that way," Tyler said, lowering his
warm, glistening body over hers . . .

Joan Darling *is a former social worker and English
teacher who now writes novels full time. She says, "I just
write—I don't wait for inspiration." Joan and her husband live near Dallas, Texas, and travel extensively;
their next trip will be to Egypt. Joan has two children
and five dogs. She enjoys playing bridge and scuba diving.*

Dear Reader:

More than one year ago, at a time when romance readers were asking for "something different," we took a bold step in romance publishing by launching an innovative new series of books about married love: TO HAVE AND TO HOLD.

Since then, TO HAVE AND TO HOLD has developed a faithful following of enthusiastic readers. We're still delighted to receive your letters—which come from teenagers, grandmothers, and women of every age in between, both married and single. All of you have one quality in common—you believe that love and romance exist beyond the "happily ever after" endings of more conventional stories.

This month we bring you *Conquer the Memories* by our very popular Jeanne Grant. Jennifer Rose also returns with *Pennies From Heaven*. And Kate Nevins, whom some of you know as the author of several SECOND CHANCE AT LOVE romances, has written her first TO HAVE AND TO HOLD, *Memory and Desire*, coming in January. Be sure, too, not to overlook the "newcomers" you'll continue to see in TO HAVE AND TO HOLD. This month Joan Darling debuts with *Tyler's Folly*, a unique, witty story that made me laugh out loud. We're proud to bring these wonderfully talented writers to you!

Warmest wishes,

Ellen Edwards

Ellen Edwards, Senior Editor
TO HAVE AND TO HOLD
The Berkley Publishing Group
200 Madison Avenue
New York, N.Y. 10016

TYLER'S FOLLY

JOAN DARLING

**SECOND CHANCE AT LOVE
BOOK**

To Have and to Hold books are published by
The Berkley Publishing Group
200 Madison Avenue, New York, NY 10016

1

HUMMING A CHEERFUL tune to boost her spirits, Gail Peabody stirred the creamy chowder simmering in the black cast-iron pot on the stove. Plump clams and bits of potato swirled around her spoon, like the anticipation and excitement swirling around inside her.

With a small smile of pleasure, she eyed a hot, golden-crusted apple pie on the counter and breathed in the yeasty aroma of bread baking in the oven as it wafted through the keeping room of the old Colonial house. A mixed green salad waited in the fridge to be tossed with creamy Italian dressing. But her heart was listening for Tyler.

Darling, good-humored, easygoing Tyler, as reliable as the steeple clock ticking on the mantel of the great stone fireplace. This was the best time of day, Gail thought, when Tyler came home. But tonight would be different.

This morning an early September frost had whitened the Connecticut countryside, signaling a change in the

weather. And always, with the ending of summer, there
came a change in the rhythm of life. This was a definite
sign, Gail decided. It was time for a change in her marriage. Once, she thought nostalgically, she and Tyler had
been as close as two peas in a pod. But now, as the
saying went, they "weren't livin' in the same pod no
more."

Yes, tonight would be different—special. She would
create an intimate, romantic ambiance about them. She
would be irresistible, provocative. She had caught up her
long black hair in a French twist and donned high heels,
and her soft gray wool dress matched her eyes and clung
to the curves of her slender figure. And keeping in mind
the old adage about the way to a man's heart, she had
prepared everything Tyler loved to eat for supper.

Brisk winds rattled the windows, sending a shiver up
her spine. Another sign? she wondered uneasily. Winds
of change?

Her heart quickened at the sound of the VW crunching
down the gravel lane. She heard the car door slam. She
ran to greet Tyler, flinging the back door wide open.

Tall, angular, wearing slightly rumpled brown tweeds,
Tyler stood grinning on the threshold, one arm bent behind his back, as if hiding something. His warm brown
eyes, the color and richness of fine sherry, brightened
at the sight of her. He curved his free arm about her narrow waist, drawing her close against his chest. A
wolfish gleam lighted his eyes. "Kiss me, woman!" he
said.

Gail wound her arms about his neck, molding her
body to his lean, lanky frame. She stood on tiptoes, eyes
closed, her moist lips slightly parted. Tyler's mouth came
down on hers in a long, fervent kiss. A tingling thrill of
excitement swept through her as her lips moved under

his in eager response. She clung to him, wanting to prolong their embrace, but Tyler drew away, breaking the enchanted moment.

A wave of disappointment surged through her. She swallowed hard, feeling suddenly deflated. Clearly, their ardent embrace was not as exciting to him as it was to her. And though he had kissed her with unusual fervor, it struck her now that his enthusiasm was forced.

She gazed up into his long, angular face, trying to read his thoughts. All she saw was a shock of straight russet hair falling over his forehead, and bristly brows arced over eyes that gave away nothing.

As she watched, his generous mouth widened in the pleased, boyish grin she found so endearing. With a flourish, he swung his arm from behind his back and handed her a green, tissue-wrapped package. "For the most beautiful woman in the world!"

Eagerly, she stripped off the paper. "Roses! And what a gorgeous shade of red! They're lovely!"

"They're Tropicanas," said Tyler affably. "I thought you'd like them."

"Oh, Tyler, you're a sweetheart!"

"I know," he agreed with disarming candor. With raised brows, he eyed the gateleg table Gail had pulled up in front of the fire blazing in the hearth and had set with a red-and-white-checked cloth, white ironstone china, and her best silver and candles. "Hey, what's the occasion?"

An inviting smile curved her full, tempting lips. "Oh, I just thought, since the weather's turned so nippy, we'd enjoy a cozy supper in front of the fire."

She crossed to the tall pine hutch, took down a pewter tankard, and filled it with water. Her heart warmed as she arranged the roses and set them in the center of the table. Had Tyler felt the rift widening between them? Was he, too, trying to recapture their former closeness?

From the corner of her eye, she watched him cross to the woodbox and lift out a log, admiring his easy, loose-limbed grace as he bent to toss it on the fire she had kindled earlier. As he stirred the flames to life, a pang of longing swept through her. If only they could rekindle the heady romance of their marriage as easily! With nervous fingers, she lighted tapered white candles set in gleaming pewter holders.

Tyler pulled two Hitchcock chairs close to the table and stood watching her, smiling his approval. In an impulsive burst of enthusiasm, he strode to the cupboard. "Let's make this a really festive occasion." He found two wineglasses, and drew a bottle of Chablis from the back of the fridge. He poured them each a glass of wine while Gail served their plates and then slid into her chair across from him.

Tyler raised his glass toward her in a smiling salute and gazed deeply into her soft gray eyes. "Here's to the future, love."

A spark of optimism flared inside her. First the flowers, and now a toast to their future. Yes, Tyler was definitely making an effort to find the way back to the way they were. Gail lifted her glass, returning his smile. "Here's to us!"

Tyler devoured his meal ravenously, praising her hearty chowder, her crusty home-baked bread, and her apple pie. They chatted amiably of this and that, sharing the events of their day. By the time they finished eating, Gail felt more lighthearted and cheerful than she had in some time. She gazed dreamily at the cluster of roses in their pewter tankard. Idly, she reached out to stroke a velvety petal. "Whatever made you think to bring me flowers, Tyler, darling?"

Tyler scraped the last crumb of pie from his plate and looked up at her, a warm, boyish grin suffusing his features. Clearly pleased with himself, he said quietly, "Today I made an executive decision—the flowers are to celebrate the occasion."

"Oh?" Basking in the warm glow of their renewed companionship, Gail heard his low, deep voice as if from far away.

"I'm going to resign from Connecticut Liberty Life."

Unable to believe the evidence of her own ears, Gail sat staring across the candlelit table at her husband of seven years as though he'd sprouted horns. At last she said faintly, "Tyler, I don't believe I heard you right. Run that past me again."

Tyler rocked back in his chair, balancing on the back legs. He placed his large, strong hands on the edge of the table and beamed at her as if he were announcing the conclusion of a million-dollar deal.

"All I said was that on November first, my fifteen-year anniversary with Connecticut Liberty Life Insurance, I'm going to hand in my resignation. Of course, I'll give them two weeks notice. I think two weeks gives them enough time to replace me, don't you?"

She wanted to say that no one in this world could ever replace him. Tyler was an original. But, unable to speak over the strangling sensation in her throat, she continued to stare at him with wide, incredulous eyes. Finally, she said, "What you're saying is, you're quitting your job, right?" She drew in a deep breath and held it.

Tyler brought his chair down with a decisive thump. "Right."

Gail let out her breath slowly. "Well, I suppose you have something else in mind, somewhere else to go." With an air of nonchalance, meant to show her confidence in whatever he'd chosen to do, she picked up her wineglass and took a sip of Chablis.

Tyler's broad, generous mouth curved in a wider grin, as if he were savoring a superb secret. "Right."

She knew he was teasing her, really itching to tell her that he'd landed some marvelous new job with some marvelous new company. He was simply enjoying leading up to his announcement, savoring his news, waiting to watch her face light up with wonder and astonishment.

Like a charge of electricity, curiosity tingled through every pore of her petite, satin-skinned body. She could scarcely wait through Tyler's usual relaxed, leisurely way of getting to the point. With an intuitive leap, her mind zeroed in on his news like an arrow flying toward a bull's-eye. After all, he was a vice-president of Connecticut Liberty Life. His leaving could only mean he'd accepted an offer as president of one of the other topnotch insurance companies in Hartford. She couldn't wait to rejoice with him, to celebrate his coup.

She set down her wineglass and leaned toward him, her lips curved in a loving smile. "Tyler Peabody, I can't wait another second. Tell me *now!* What are you going to do? Where are you going?"

He reached across the table and clasped her slender hands in his large, warm palms. His warm brown eyes glistened with excitement. His lean, open, honest face glowed with pleasure and anticipation.

"I'm going to live on a desert island."

Gail's mouth dropped open. As though mesmerized, her eyes clung to Tyler's. She shook her head, laughing.

"Come on, darling. I can't stand the suspense. Where are you going to work?"

With a reproachful glance, as if affronted by her disbelief, he withdrew his hands from hers and took up his favorite Meerschaum pipe. With slow deliberation, he stuffed it with tobacco, tamped it down, and lighted it. In calm, quiet tones he said, "I'm not going to work. I'm going to live on a desert island."

Gail let out a sigh of mingled exasperation and resignation. *Talking* about going to live on a desert island was not *going*. With an affable grin, she said, "Okay, Tyler. *Nobody* retires at age thirty-seven, and I'm not exactly on the shelf at twenty-six, but if you want to kid around, tell me about your pipe dream."

Tyler drew deeply on his pipe. He blew a perfect circle of fragrant, spicy smoke toward the beamed ceiling, then met her eyes with a level, direct gaze. "I kid you not. I've thought about this for a long while. With my anniversary bonus check, I'll buy tickets to somewhere and make a Great Escape from the corporate rat race."

Panic rose in her throat, threatening to choke her. For an instant, Gail thought her heart would stop beating. Then she could hear it, pounding in her ears. And she could hear the steeple clock ticking loudly on the mantel of the great fieldstone fireplace, and the fire crackling in the hearth, and a floorboard in the huge old white frame house creaking in the heavy silence that hung between them.

Flabbergasted, she stared at Tyler. For the first time, she noticed the bleak, tired expression in the depths of his eyes, the fine lines of strain about his mouth. His angular face blurred, wavering in the candlelight. His lips seemed to stretch in an ever-widening smile. His white, rust, and blue paisley tie shimmered against the snowy whiteness of his shirt, and his tweed-clad shoulders seemed to expand. The irreverent thought struck her that she should have known something horrible was about to happen, known it was a sign of disaster when he lighted his tobacco, for he unfailingly puffed on an empty pipe.

A feeling of desolation overwhelmed her. All during the long years Tyler had traveled from Monday to Friday, she had kept busy and cheerful sculpting and working with the Animal Rescue League and Friends of the Zoo. Now, winning blue ribbons in local art shows was no longer fulfilling. After Tyler's promotion to the home office three months ago, she had looked forward to the return of their old intimacy. Instead, for all she saw of him, he might still be traveling like the proverbial Yankee peddler.

She had told herself that as soon as Tyler adjusted to his new job, their new routine, they would recapture the old warmth and camaraderie they had once shared. She just had to give him time to adjust. But as the days dragged by, she and Tyler lived like two ships that passed in the night, and she had concluded that Tyler didn't really need her. And she needed to be needed.

No, she thought grimly, Tyler didn't need her at all, except for those delicious, delightful, delirious times when they were both overwhelmed with a passion to possess each other fully and completely. Her heart soared with remembered joy. They had always found time for love-making.

Noisily, Tyler cleared his throat, claiming her attention. With a show of blasé aplomb, he was blowing an endless, incredible series of smoke rings upward.

She tried to make her voice calm and reasonable, but it came out in a high-pitched squeak. "Escape from the corporate rat race, you say—as if you hadn't slaved to climb to the top of the corporate pyramid!"

Tyler nodded. Between gauzy wreaths of smoke, he muttered, "I've reached the peak. The challenge is gone."

Harebrained as his idea seemed, she knew if she kicked up a fuss, he'd be all the more determined to go through with it. Anyway, what did *she* know? She might *love* life on a desert island. And she knew that in the end, he'd charm her into going along. Tyler Peabody could sell vacuum cleaners to desert tribesmen. She gave Tyler a radiant smile, raised her glass in salute, and swallowed another sip of Chablis.

"Well, Tyler, if that's your decision, I'm with you all the way. When and where will we go?"

Tyler's chain of smoke rings broke off abruptly. In gentle tones, he replied, "I'm going alone."

"Tyler!" she shrieked, slapping her wineglass down on the table. Plainly, all that pipe-smoking had gone to his head. "You *can't* be serious!"

"I was never more serious in my life." With a noble, self-sacrificing air, he went on: "I wouldn't dream of asking you—I have no right to ask you—to give up the life you've carved out for yourself here at home to go tripping off to a desert island with me."

"But, Tyler, making you happy is what I most want to do in this world. I love you! I love you as much as the day we were married—*more* than the day we were married. I want to be with you!"

Tyler gazed at her fondly. He set down his pipe, reached out, and clasped her cold hands in his. "And I love you, darling. That's one more reason why I must go, and go alone, so we can reach the full potential of our lives. I know you haven't been really happy since my promotion to the home office. This will give you a chance to be all you *can* be. You'll sculpt and I'll seek out my true niche in this world on some South Seas island."

"But, Tyler!" she wailed. "Even the Prix de Rome would mean nothing without you!"

Tyler released her hands and placed a gentle finger on her quivering lips. "You're not to worry about a thing, love. I've invested our money wisely, so you can continue to live here comfortably on the income, in the style to which you're accustomed."

"Hold on, Tyler!" she burst out. "Remember, *you* are accustomed to this style, too!"

Tyler picked up his pipe and with devastating determination replied, "I will become accustomed to a new style."

"Tyler," Gail said with deadly calm, "I can become accustomed to a new style just as well as you can."

An expression of genuine regret filled his eyes.

"Gail, the last thing in the world I want to do is hurt you, but I *need* to go alone. You'll get along fine without me, just as you did when I traveled. You needn't worry about the house. I've raked up the leaves, mulched the gardens, and chopped and stacked another cord of oak for the fireplaces. I'll put up the storm windows before I take off, and I've already stashed the lawn furniture in the barn."

"What about the cars?" asked Gail hopefully. "You can't abandon our old cars. They'll never make it through the winter!"

"I've cleaned up the junk in the barn. There's plenty of room for the station wagon *and* the VW. I even managed to squeeze in the outdoor grill."

Struck speechless, Gail thought: He's *planned* all this! Thought it all out! He's really going! He'd never taken much interest in maintaining things, and she had thought his recent zeal was very encouraging. But all the time he was mulching and chopping and cleaning out the barn he was planning his Great Escape!

For a long moment, her lips refused to speak the devastating thought that sprang to her mind. Had he ceased to love her? When at last she managed a ragged whisper, she was unable to ask the question scalding her heart. Instead, she asked, "Does this mean we'll never see each other again?"

Tyler's broad palm swept through the air in a magnanimous gesture. "Of course not!"

A shaky laugh escaped her. "I have to hand it to you, Tyler. You have style, saying it with flowers." Taking a deep breath, she forced herself to speak the unspeakable. "You're really asking for a divorce."

Tyler's hand halted in midair, his eyes widening in startled astonishment.

"Divorce!" he shouted, in appalled tones, leaping up from his chair. "Divorce is *not* what this is about." He ran his hands through his straight sandy hair, pacing the floor like a restless tiger. "It's about how I feel locked in, trapped in the corporate jungle. There has to be more to life than commuting to Hartford, hopping on a train every morning, working like the devil all day, feeling like a pressure cooker ready to blow, falling asleep on the train coming home, then plunging into paper work every night after dinner. You should read Rousseau, darling." His eyes lighted up with a lofty, dreamy expression. "He believed in self-expression instead of regimentation. He stressed the value of feelings as opposed to reason, and of impulse and spontaneity instead of self-discipline and restraint. He knew how to live life to the fullest. 'Natural' man is much better off than 'civilized' man.'" In jubilant tones, Tyler announced, "I'm going to be one of Rousseau's 'children of nature.'"

"Down with Rousseau!" Gail burst out. She took another deep breath to calm herself. "Well, then, how long will you be gone?"

He leaned toward her and reached out, patting her shoulder consolingly. "Who can say how long it will take a man to find himself..."

"But, Tyler, you can't mean you'd go tripping off forever!"

Tyler looked pained. His shoulders lifted in a helpless shrug, his hands outstretched in an imploring gesture. "Try to understand, darling. I don't want to be pinned down—that's one reason I'm going. No pressures, no schedules, and no restrictions, no regimentation, no routines to stick to..."

In quiet, sympathetic tones, she said, "I do understand, Tyler." She understood that he wanted his freedom. And because she understood, she could think of no defense. In benumbed silence, she watched him heave another log on the low-burning fire and poke it into life just as if this were any other ordinary evening. But instead of turning away and charging into his study to work, he searched through a box of tapes, slipped one into the cassette player, and turned it on. Then he sank down in the Lincoln rocker and stared dreamily into the fire, where blazing gold flames were licking around the logs like rampant lions, leaping up the wide stone chimney as if escaping to freedom.

Dolefully, Gail thought of all the ways she might have reacted to Tyler's declaration of independence. She could have pitched a fit; wept hysterically; shouted at him, enraged; tossed her wine in his face; dumped the roses over his innocent, well-intentioned head. Instead, she sat like a lump of clay, doing nothing, knowing that whatever she did, Tyler would remain unmoved, undaunted, undeterred in his purpose.

Staring thoughtfully at Tyler relaxing in his rocker, she said softly, "You know, Tyler, you can at times be rather mule-headed." Lost in his reverie, Tyler appeared not to hear her. "Like the time you fell in love with that rocker at a farm auction. Even though you knew that a Lincoln rocker was much too new to deserve house room with our antique pine and maple furniture, you were a bidding fool till the rocker was yours." The memory made her smile. She never could throw cold water on his enthusiasm, never could deny him anything he wanted.

As the sweet, haunting, romantic strains of *Elvira Madigan,* one of their favorite recordings, flowed through the room, Gail felt like bursting into tears. Was Tyler playing "their song" to etch it into his memory before leaving all she thought he had held near and dear?

"Tyler," she asked softly, in a voice that throbbed with emotion, "how can you endure to leave our lovely hills and valleys? Won't you miss our dazzling show of color in the fall? Our soft snows so perfect for skiing and tobogganing in winter? The hope and promise of our fresh, green spring? Our soft, warm summer days, and your garden? You take such pride in your rosebeds and marigolds and zinnias, and your vegetable patch, your rows of string beans and sweet corn and tomatoes. Won't you miss all that?"

"Yes," replied Tyler bravely. "But there will be compensations..."

As if he hadn't spoken, Gail went on. "Not to mention your home, the very house you've grown up in, echoing with memories of your happy childhood!"

Tyler's lips curved in a wry smile. "It's hard to hear

echoes when you're an only child and have read your way through childhood. Besides, 'Man will endure!' Faulkner," he added confidently, quoting from one of his favorite authors.

How could she argue with Faulkner? And how she wished Tyler did not know a quote for every occasion. Through lids brimming with tears, Gail gazed about the spacious kitchen they called the keeping room, as though seeing it for the last time. Beside Tyler's rocker on the round pedestal table rested a huge glass bowl, home of J. Alfred Prufrock, Tyler's giant goldfish; and there lay Tyler's *New York Times* crossword puzzle and the pen with which he worked it; and the book he was reading by Jean-Jacques Rousseau.

Her gaze roved past wavy-paned windows hung with white ruffled curtains, where pots of African violets bloomed in gay profusion on the sill; the iridescent, blue-green bouquet of peacock feathers she had brought from the zoo for Tyler's antique tin milk can by the door; their collection of pewter candlesticks, tankards, and plates gleaming with the soft patina of age gracing the shelves of the massive pine hutch they had refinished when they were first married. A lump rose in her throat. All she had done to make a warm and loving home for Tyler meant nothing to him!

An overwhelming feeling of nostalgia swept through her. "Tyler, don't you sometimes wish back our newly-wed days when we were poor as church mice, living in a tiny apartment? Remember how thrilled and excited we were when we bought the old scarred hutch? How elated we were the day we found our four-poster bed, and later, this gateleg table and the Hitchcock chairs, and the weatherbeaten walnut chest of drawers in the parlor?"

Tyler grinned, cocking an eyebrow. "And remember all our blood, sweat, and toil refinishing them?"

"But we had fun together, Tyler, stripping, scraping, and sanding, waxing and polishing each piece to a satin sheen. Don't you remember all the joy and pride and satisfaction we felt in creating beautiful things for our home?"

"'You can't go home again,'" Tyler murmured. "Wolfe. Can't live in the past."

"I know." Gail let out a long, loud sigh. No longer did they dash off to farm sales and auctions like prospectors searching for gold, for Tyler was too busy climbing the ladder of success. They had enough gold, and more than enough furniture with an attic crammed full of antiques handed down from both their families. And now, thought Gail, dismally, the intimate supper and cozy evening she had planned on this first frost-bitten day of September had gone dead like the ashes of yesterday's fire.

A scratching at the back door roused her from her dour thoughts. Mechanically, she rose from the table and opened the door. On a wave of cold air, Sidney, their black Siberian Husky, boasting a handsome white mask and ears, burst inside and bounded about the room. After winning an abstracted pat on the head from Tyler, he sat at Gail's feet, his plumed tail wagging. An expectant gleam shone from his light eyes, one brown, the other blue, which Gail felt gave him a certain distinction.

An unprecedented surge of affection for Sidney flowed through her. *He* would never desert her, she thought, with a reproachful glance at Tyler. She had never intended to keep Sidney when she brought him home from the zoo after his mother's death during dog birth. But by the time he was old enough to return to the zoo, a new acquisition, a hyena, had been stashed in his den, and there was no room for Sidney. Now, she was grateful for his company. She knelt down and gave him a hug, resting her head on his thick ruff. He licked her cheek affectionately.

Abruptly, she rose and dumped dog food into Sidney's bowl. By the time she had cleared the table, she had recovered some of her composure. Plunging her hands into hot, soapy dishwater brought her to her senses. No one in his right mind would do what Tyler planned!

Of course, she could try to reason with him. Or she could tell him how she herself felt like a hollow woman, yet was not copping out, taking off to parts unknown. Or she could tell him how unneeded she felt. If she'd had any doubts as to whether or not Tyler needed her, she thought gloomily, he had certainly confirmed them. But *now* was definitely not the time to bring up her own feelings. Tyler might think she was pleading with him not to leave. Heartbroken she might be, but her New England born-and-bred pride was stronger. She would never beg him to stay with her against his will.

The smell of woodsmoke in the air, the sudden cold snap, brought back precious memories of their annual bittersweet hunt heralding the onset of fall. Happiness flowed through her as she recalled their last jaunt into the countryside. In a gay, carefree mood, they had reveled in the beauty of the brilliant tapestry of hills and valleys ablaze with magnificent hues of scarlet, yellow, spice brown, copper, and wine. They had stopped beside an orchard on a hillside and picked crisp, red juicy apples to munch along the way. In midafternoon, they had lunched at a romantic old country inn, and afterward gathered a huge bunch of bittersweet. At the day's end, they had felt exhilarated, renewed. When they got home,

Gail arranged the scarlet berries in a low Chinese brass bowl and set it on the walnut chest in the front parlor, a cheerful, winter-long reminder of the joy of their outing.

Gail dried her hands on a towel and crossed to stand before Tyler, who was sitting with his head back, eyes closed, dreaming in his rocker. She gazed down at him, a look of longing in her soft gray eyes. "Well, darling," she said quietly, "since you're rebelling against regimentation, I suppose you don't care to go on our annual bittersweet hunt."

She was gratified to see his eyes fly open, and an indignant, incredulous expression suffusing his good-natured features.

"Of course I want to go!" he shouted. "Why wouldn't I? Wouldn't miss it for the world!"

"Are you *sure?* I wouldn't want you to go if you don't really want to."

"Of course I'm sure. You know I enjoy riding out in the country as much as you do. In fact, we'll go tomorrow!"

Her lips curved in a ravishing smile. One minute he was talking of an imminent departure to a South Seas island; the next minute, he was clinging to their old, familiar rituals. Plainly, her dreamer husband did not know his own mind. But she knew *her* own mind. The only thing to do was nip in the bud this noxious weed of discontent that had sprung up in the smooth green lawn of their lives. She would begin with their bittersweet hunt.

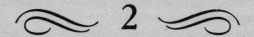

2

On Saturday afternoon, riding beside Tyler in the VW with the top down, along winding blacktop roads, Gail marveled that everything seemed peachy-keen between them. To look at them—she in her neat navy blue blazer, white pullover, and gray slacks, Tyler in his creamy turtleneck sweater and natty brown cords—who would guess that her faithful, dependable, devoted husband was on the verge of abandoning her, maybe forever? It wouldn't bear thinking about.

The air was fresh and clear and vibrant. The sun, hung in a blue gentian sky, shone with a brilliance that warmed her body, thawing the frozen feeling inside her. She gazed appreciatively about her, admiring the countryside drenched with golden light.

"Like a Gauguin painting," Tyler observed happily. "We couldn't have asked for a better day!"

Not caring for the direction his thoughts were taking, with Gauguin in the South Seas, Gail said nothing. She had looked forward to their outing with a mixture of anticipation and dread—anticipation at the chance to relive their former forays into the country in happier days; dread that this might be the last display of breathtaking fall foliage they would ever see together.

This morning at breakfast a heart-stopping feeling of being like a condemned woman taking her last walk to the guillotine had engulfed her. She had told Tyler she thought they should cancel their outing. "After all," she said sadly, "you won't be here to enjoy the bittersweet through the long, cold winter."

Tyler had protested vehemently. "Our bittersweet hunt is a tradition. We must go! I insist! We owe it to ourselves!"

Now, she was glad they were here. Maybe reliving happy memories of their former outings would bring Tyler down to earth, back to the *real* world, would reawaken him to the joys of life in Connecticut so he would give up his ridiculous plan.

Tyler drove the VW at a leisurely speed along lazy, curving roads, through colorful patchwork hills and valleys dotted with white houses and red barns; past meandering streams and quiet ponds and low fieldstone walls guarding grassy meadows abloom with spiky goldenrod and yellow-starred amethyst asters. At length, the VW crested a long, sloping hill. Gail's heart leaped as she gazed down into the valley hugging the river.

"Tyler! There's *our* inn!"

At the foot of the hill, a stone's throw from the banks of the river, nestled among tall pines, mountain laurel, crimson maples, and winey-leafed dogwood, sprawled a rambling red brick inn. Dormer windows and a massive chimney dominated the black mansard roof.

An aching wave of nostalgia flooded through her.

Here they had spent their honeymoon. And here their marriage might end. Had Tyler deliberately brought her here? Was this his way of winding down, bringing their marriage full circle? She longed for him to say something—anything—to show that he, too, was touched by sight of the charming country inn where they had once known such joy.

"Yep," said Tyler in matter-of-fact tones. "There it is. It's been standing there for two hundred years—and will probably stand for two hundred more."

Gail swallowed her disappointment. Sentiment was not one of Tyler's strong points. To jog his memory, she said warmly, "Remember our honeymoon, darling? Making love in the tester bed..."

"...and the bed broke down, and we got all tangled up in the fishnet canopy!" Tyler chuckled, giving a rueful shake of his head. "Those old rope beds were never meant to hold innerspring mattresses."

Or, thought Gail wistfully, to hold newlyweds making love with such wild abandon. She said no more until they had parked the car and strolled through the lobby into the spacious, high-ceilinged dining room. Gold damask draperies graced the windows. Gilt-framed landscapes adorned white walls where gleaming brass sconces bloomed with yellow candlelight. The maître d' seated them before the stately Palladian window overlooking the river.

"Tyler!" exclaimed Gail. "We sat at this same table on our honeymoon! *Remember?*" Her soft gray eyes glowed with delight. Surely this was a sign that their marriage would begin anew, take on new life and meaning.

Tyler stared thoughtfully out the window at the shiny, placid, slow-moving waters flowing past. His face lit up.

"I don't remember this table, but I do remember fishing from the riverbank. You fell in and pulled me in after you."

An embarrassed flush crept up Gail's cheeks into her hairline.

"That was because you kept fishing for something besides bass, darling. You needed a good dunking to cool your insatiable, unbridled passions."

She felt suddenly cheered by the thought that Tyler's passions remained, to this day, insatiable and unbridled. She reached across the table and placed her hand in his. Her heart swelled with joy as his fingers closed around hers in a warm clasp and he smiled deeply, lovingly, into her eyes.

The tender moment was interrupted by the waiter, who took their order and left. A sudden burst of music filled the air. Their heads turned to a balcony at the far end of the room where a string quartet swung into a sprightly Chopin waltz, setting a gay, festive mood. Things are looking up, Gail thought, elated.

Their meal was no less elegant than their surroundings. In a heady ambiance of pure pleasure, enhanced by several glasses of light white Chardonnay, they dined on shrimp cocktails, Boston scrod, asparagus tips smothered in hollandaise sauce, fresh mushrooms, and corn fritters, along with chef's salad and hot garlic bread. For dessert, they splurged on a puffy, lighter-than-air soufflé, with a chaser of crème de menthe. The sun was well over the yardarm by the time they settled themselves in the car again. Gail felt lighter than air. Tyler whistled a cheerful tune as he steered the VW down the narrow, curving road.

As they wound their leisurely way past a stretch of woodland redolent with the musty odor of fallen leaves, it was Tyler whose keen, discerning eye first spotted the bright red berries. The woody vines crept along the ground and up the trunk of a gnarled elm. Great clusters of scarlet berries cloaked in orange husks, with curling, heart-shaped leaves, clung to the naked branches.

. Tyler braked to a stop by the side of the road. They clambered from the car. Heads bent, they scuffled through an ankle-deep drift of leaves searching for the thickest, fullest vines. Tyler pulled up a strand. "How's this?"

Gail pursed her lips. "I don't think they'll last through the winter. The husks have opened too wide for the berries to be fresh." Her eager, speculative gaze traveled upward to the vines clinging to the knotted limbs of the old elm. "Those look much thicker and heartier."

Tyler appeared skeptical. Gail's bright, hopeful eyes locked with his. "Okay, I'll climb up and get them for you."

Quickly, she reached out and put a hand on his arm. "No, Tyler, you're too heavy, the limbs won't hold you. I'll climb up. I'm a natural. You may be a Peabody, but I'm descended from chimpanzees." Ignoring his protests, she threw off her navy blazer, kicked off her shoes, wrapped her arms around the rough-barked trunk, and shinnied up the tree.

"Be careful, for heaven's sake!" yelled Tyler. "Don't go any higher!"

"Don't worry. I'm afraid of heights, remember? I only want to get one nice clump just beyond this fork in the limb."

Straddling the sturdy limb, she crept cautiously along, easing beyond the fork toward the tempting cluster of berries. She reached out and wrenched the tough vine from its moorings, twisting off strands and tossing them down on the bed of leaves below.

Tyler stood watching her, his head thrown back, nervously jiggling the change in his pockets. "Come on, you have enough, let's go."

"Just one more clump!" She inched farther along, leaning forward and reaching toward the elusive berries. Her stomach lurched as she felt the branch sway under her slight weight. She yanked the vine toward her. With a mighty tug, she tore off a length and dropped it. It landed on Tyler's upturned face.

Laughing, he disentangled himself. "Enough!" he shouted. "Get down here, woman!"

"I am, I am. Hold your horses!"

Hunched over the limb, she gripped it with both hands and started to back up slowly toward the trunk. Too late, she realized she'd inched dangerously far out, and with each movement of her body, the branch gave a sickening sway.

"Turn around!" Tyler shouted excitedly. "Throw your weight forward! Quit going ass-backward!"

Her hands, suddenly moist and clammy, froze to the swaying limb. "I can't!"

"Well, then let go. Just drop straight down. You're only fifteen feet from the ground. I'll catch you."

Gail peered down through the network of bare branches. Tyler's agitated face stared up at her, his arms flung wide. From where she sat, he looked miles away. A tremor of fear spiraled through her. "I can't. I'm going to lie down on my back and wiggle across..."

"The hell you are!" Tyler shouted, stripping off his corduroy jacket. "Hang on. I'm coming up after you."

With a swiftness and agility that astonished her, Tyler scaled the trunk and straddled the listing limb, six feet behind her. He stretched out an arm, as if offering an oar to a drowning victim.

"Grab hold. I'll steady you while you turn around."

Cautiously, she maneuvered the upper half of her body clockwise, reaching for his hand. Their fingertips almost touched. She leaned toward him, arching her back. Her fingers brushed his. She could see the veins in his temples swell as he strained to reach her. The dry, brittle limb creaked and swayed under their double weight. Beads of sweat popped out on Tyler's forehead. Through clenched jaws, he muttered, "You'll have to come to me. If I go any farther, the damned limb will give way."

Her mouth grew dry. She clutched the swaying branch, and with an effort of will hitched back another inch, then stretched an arm toward Tyler.

With a jubilant cry, he seized her hand. "Gotcha! Now, start turning. Throw your leg over, pretend you're riding sidesaddle. Easy does it."

In slow motion, she swung her left leg over and curled both hands around the limb. "I feel like a bird perched on a wire—and I'm dizzy!" She shook her head to clear it.

"Don't look down," Tyler commanded. "Just look at me. Turn and shift your right leg over. Start scooching toward me. Easy, now!"

She kept her eyes fixed on Tyler's anxious face. With one hand clutched securely in his, the other balancing her weight on the limb before her, she bumped along, caterpillar fashion. At last they met, nose to nose.

"Right on!" Tyler cried. "That's my girl!"

"Oh, Tyler, I was sure I'd fall on my head!" In a flush of exuberance, she threw her arms around his neck in a gigantic bear hug. Taken by surprise, Tyler let go his hold on the limb and wrapped his arms about her, clutching her tightly against his chest. The next instant, they were plummeting through space.

"Oof!" Tyler exploded, as they struck the ground, their fall cushioned by the thick quilt of leaves.

Tyler lay limply on his back, Gail sprawled across his chest.

"Tyler!" she cried, in a voice sharp with fear. "Are you hurt?"

He groaned softly. "You knocked the wind out of me! That's all."

"Oh, Tyler, I'm sorry, I thought you had a good grip on me."

He managed a wry grin. "I did. It was the branch I didn't have a good grip on. I may soar like an eagle, but I'm short on talons." A concerned expression came into his eyes. "How about you, darling? You okay?"

"I think so."

"No bones broken?"

He rose to his knees and ran his hands down her arms, pressing each bone with gentle care, sliding down hip and thigh with the same tender touch. He rolled her onto her side, bending down to feel the bones of her slender ankles and feet. As if reassured, his fingers skipped upward, playfully poking here and there.

Gail grinned. "I'm okay, really, Tyler."

Undaunted, he continued to explore. "Ribs intact? One, two, three...Oops, I've lost count!" Gently, he kneaded her high, firm breasts.

At the passionate way he was looking at her, through half-lidded eyes, she felt a warm wave of love flood through her. A challenging, mischievous gleam lighted her gray eyes.

"Don't start anything you're not willing to finish, Tyler." She caught his powerful wrists in her hands, holding them tight. Grinning, she said, "You're overdoing it, Doctor. I *told* you, everything's okay."

"You can say that again!" He twisted free. His arms encircled her waist. He stretched out beside her, pulling her to him, so they were lying face to face, hip to hip. "How about your back?"

A delicious shiver tingled through her as his strong fingers stroked the back of her neck, then strayed down the slender column of her spine, circling each vertebra. She felt her body relaxing, melting like tallow. His hands curved over her haunches, closing firmly around them, drawing her tightly against him. His breath, like fresh mint, was soft on her cheek. She breathed in the scent of his body, like freshly laundered sheets blown dry on a clothesline on a windy day. She could feel her own body responding, warming, welcoming, opening to his.

She wished they were home, snuggling in their four-poster bed. Home, where they could make love far into the night until sated, then fall asleep in each other's arms. Maybe their romantic mood would hold. Tyler's lips, soft, seeking, probed hers. She mustn't let herself go, must hold on just long enough to make it home, to the four-poster, where they could let their passions have free reign.

She tore her lips from his and sat up. In a tremulous whisper, she said, "Let's go home!"

A teasing light came into his eyes. "I'm not ready to go home. You said not to start something I'm not willing to finish."

A seductive, provocative smile curved her full, moist lips. "I know."

He sat up and began brushing bits of bark and twigs from her soft white sweater. He picked yellowed leaves from her hair, smoothing it back, sliding his palms down the long, glossy black strands. Grinning, he said, "Your hairdo is ruined."

Gail laughed. "So is yours, but I love you anyway."

His arms closed around her. A mischievous glint came into her eyes. She slipped from his grasp, jumped up, scooped up an armful of crisp, dry leaves, and dumped them over his head. As though the sky had fallen, Tyler leaped to his feet. A look of utter astonishment contorted his usually calm countenance.

Gail burst out laughing, arms folded across her chest, bent at the waist, convulsed. "Oh, Tyler, you look so funny!"

She was still laughing when a sudden shower of leaves tumbled down over her own head. Tyler's loud, boisterous laughter mingled with her own.

Like dervishes, they whirled through the golden dusk, laughing, shouting, scooping up leaves, tossing them skyward. The soft autumn air swirled with a blizzard of brittle rust, yellow, and wine-red leaves. Without warning, Gail spun away from Tyler and, like a doe in flight, ran deep into the woodland.

Tyler's howl of outrage echoed after her. "Come back here, you leafhopper!" She heard a scuffling noise and thudding footsteps striking the ground as Tyler pounded in pursuit.

Breathless, gasping, she emerged in a grassy clearing ringed by great white oaks, giant red maples, wine-leafed dogwood, and a scattering of rich green pines. She started at the sound of a bloodcurdling victory whoop from the woods behind her. The next instant, two powerful arms closed around her, pinning her against a lean, sinewy body. Gail let out a shriek. A cottontail rabbit bolted for cover.

Laughing, squirming against Tyler's muscular chest, Gail shrieked, "What do you think you're doing, tackling me like some halfback!"

In a tangle of arms and legs, Tyler wrestled her to the ground, panting, "Didn't I ever tell you I played quarterback for M.I.T.?"

"But, Tyler, we're not playing football!"

Tyler chuckled. "Don't worry. M.I.T. doesn't *have* a football team. And *I'm* not playing football either." With one smooth motion, he rolled her on her back and flung his lean, lanky length on top of her. His mouth closed over hers, insistent, demanding, like a parched traveler drinking from a pool at a desert oasis.

Gail felt warm and loving. Her arms curved about Tyler's neck. Her fingers strayed through his thick, straight hair, down the back of his neck, under his collar, stroking his skin. He peeled off his shirt, and quickly, expertly, stripped off her T-shirt and bra and cast them aside. She felt her nipples grow taut with desire. Her breasts swelled with longing. She pressed closer against his hairy chest. A delicious languor flowed throughout her body like golden, honey-sweet syrup from the first spring tap of the sugar maples. With light, feathery kisses, he covered her brows, her eyelids, her cheeks, the dimple in her chin, her soft, eager lips.

She looked up into his face. His eyes were closed and a look of devotion, of reverence, suffused his flushed features. A shaft of sunlight sifting through lacy-leafed oaks shed a golden ambiance on the grassy glen. Somewhere a meadowlark called, its song mingling with the soft babble of a nearby stream.

Tyler shifted his weight and, rising on his knees, eased off the rest of her clothes, along with his own. A mild breeze rippled over her, making her naked flesh tingle. Gently Tyler lowered his body over hers. She closed her eyes, reveling in the touch of his big gentle hands caressing her body, arousing in her a ravenous hunger that only he could satisfy.

He cupped a hand behind her head and loosened the scarlet ribbon that bound her hair, running his fingers through the dark satin spill that flowed free. Braced on his elbows, he folded his arms under her head, pillowing it on his forearms. His lips assaulted hers with deep, passionate kisses.

"Tyler!" she gasped. "Tyler, darling!"

Tyler's lips moved demandingly over hers. "Gail, my sweet, my love," he murmured huskily, "we must do this more often!"

Hungrily, she responded to his turbulent kisses. He continued his slow, sensuous stroking in all the secret places, stirring her senses to a peak of passionate desire.

She twisted her hips in a slow, undulating, sensuous rhythm, arching her back, pressing her body frantically into the curve of his embrace. His hands cupped around her hips, drawing her closer. She felt as though she were drowning in his love as he pressed her down, down, down upon the soft, loamy earth.

He bent his head to hers, kissing her everywhere so that all the bright leaves overhead and on the ground around them swirled about her in a vivid kaleidoscope of color. She no longer heard the song of the meadowlark or the babbling stream. She neither knew nor cared that she and Tyler lay naked under the sun. Sunlight danced on their gleaming skin. The soft, earthy woodland fragrance of sweetfern and pine eddied around them.

"Your hair smells like roses," Tyler murmured, "and your breasts are like creamy velvet petals." His lips closed full and warm over hers, his body heat mingling with her own as he whispered words of love in ardent, breathless tones of mounting passion.

With a slow, sensuous touch, his knowledgeable hands explored the shape of her body, caressing, possessing every curve and crevice with an ardor that ignited the fires smoldering within her. His breath came faster. He opened his eyes and gazed at her with a wild, burning intensity. Desire exploded inside her. In a frenzy of passion their bodies fused. An ecstatic cry escaped her. Pleasure suffused her senses, tingling along every nerve ending. Her arms tightened about him. As she clasped him closer, ever closer, she felt a tremendous shudder course through the length of his body, as though he were shaken to the depths by an emotion greater than any man could contain. When at last their lusty passions were sated, they lay, bodies entwined, in a rapturous warmth, adrift in a dreamlike euphoria that seemed to have no end.

Gail had no idea how long they lay in the leaves in the golden dusk steeped in the languor of their lovemaking. Cool air stippling their bodies roused them.

Driving home through the gathering dusk, Tyler and Gail were silent, each immersed in thought. Gail surfaced slowly, reluctantly. She had relived every rapturous moment of their lovemaking, engraving each one in her heart.

She tried to sort out her thoughts and feelings. For one thing, she was astonished that her conservative, conventional Tyler would take her, stark naked, in the middle of a woodland glen in broad daylight. Suppressing a smile, she concluded once again that there was more to Tyler than met the eye. His astonishing behavior this afternoon, along with his flaky notion of going native on a desert island, was a definite sign of something, but what? Maybe he was suffering from some sort of personality change. Or was he? Maybe she had never known the *real* Tyler! Had she married a wolf in sheepskin? A tiger in catskin? She cast him a sidelong glance.

He drove with his hands firmly on the wheel, his eyes intent on the road ahead. His features bore his customary good-natured expression. As she watched, a sudden smile quirked the corners of his mouth. Was he, too, reliving their blissful hour in the sunlit glen?

She leaned her head back against the seat and closed her eyes, reveling in the memory of Tyler's healing touch, balm to her bruised and battered ego. She smiled to herself. Of one thing she was certain. After this afternoon, Tyler would never leave her.

When they arrived home, they had a light, leisurely supper, and afterward, instead of working, Tyler turned on the stereo and played their favorite music. At ten o'clock, when Tyler took Sidney for his nightly stroll, Gail arranged the crimson-berried bittersweet in a Chinese brass bowl and set it on the walnut chest in the front parlor, then stood back to admire the effect. Tyler came into the room and crossed to her side. Resting his chin on her hair, he draped an arm about her shoulders and gave her a little hug.

"The parlor wouldn't look right without our bittersweet," he said, gazing in admiration at her handiwork. He reached out a hand, snapped off a sprig of berries, and tucked it behind his ear. He bent his head and kissed the dimple in her chin. Softly, he whispered, "'A thing of beauty is a joy forever: its loveliness increases; it will never pass into nothingness; but still will keep a bower quiet for us, and a sleep full of sweet dreams, and health, and quiet breathing.' Keats."

Touched by his words, she couldn't speak, but looked

up into his face, love shining from her eyes.

"Let's go to bed," Tyler murmured.

Gail's heart swelled with happiness. A feeling of utter peace and contentment came over her. Tradition had triumphed. The closeness she and Tyler once shared had returned. Tyler would stay home. All was right with her world.

Curled spoon fashion about Tyler's sinewy body in their four-poster bed, Gail snuggled closer against his broad back, warming her feet against his hirsute calves. He had kindled a fire in the fireplace, and a low, steady flame crackled in the hearth, spreading its warmth about the chill room.

She was drifting off to sleep when she heard Tyler murmur, "Maybe I shouldn't go off to a desert island in the South Seas after all."

A wide, knowing smile curved her lips, but she said nothing.

In deep, thoughtful tones he rambled on. "It's tempting to go to Tahiti and live like Rousseau's child of nature; but maybe I'd rather go to Wyoming and live on a meadow in a sheepherder's wagon; or to the Sahara and live like a nomad, sleeping in a tent and roaming the sweeping sands on camelback."

A mélange of horror and disbelief swept through her. He must be dreaming! She rose to her knees and, gripping Tyler's shoulders, gave him a vigorous shake. "Tyler! Wake up! You're having a nightmare!"

He rolled over. In the glow of the flickering firelight, Gail saw a startled, questioning expression shining from his eyes.

"Wrong!" Tyler said affably. "I'm ruminating."

"Well, stop ruminating right now!" she cried hysterically. "It's a bunch of nonsense. After all the fun we had today, how can you even ruminate about leaving!"

Tyler sat up in bed, gazing at her with an injured air. "But, Gail, darling, that's why I insisted we go on our annual outing—to make our final foray into the country together. That's why I'm so happy that today was utterly perfect! It's a memory I'll always treasure; it's etched in my mind forever. I even saved a sprig of bittersweet to take with me, a memento. On days when I'm sated with the sybaritic life, with the warm green and blue seas, the palm-studded, white-sand beaches, and beautiful natives, I will hold it in my hand, and look at it, and relive this wonderful day with you."

Incredulous, Gail stared into the face of this stranger in her bed. His sincere, determined gaze locked with hers. In choked tones, she whispered, "You're hell-bent on going, aren't you?"

Relentlessly, Tyler nodded.

A feeling of utter desolation overwhelmed her. She covered her face with her hands and burst into tears.

Tyler reached out and drew her close to his chest, pressing her head against his shoulder, smoothing her soft, curling hair. In deep, soothing tones, he crooned, "Don't cry, darling. You'll be all right. Don't worry."

"I'm not worried about me," she said, sniffing. "I'm worried about you."

"Oh, I'll be just great," said Tyler in tones far too jovial to reassure her. "And you'll be better off, too, in the long run. It couldn't be pleasant for you to live with a malcontent like me, a monster, snarling day and night."

She gazed up at him, eyes imploring, tears glistening on her softly rounded cheeks. "Let's give it a go."

With an air of finality, Tyler shook his head. "Gail, you have to understand that there are certain things in a man's life he must do. This is a thing *I* must do. We'll say no more about it." Gently, he eased her down on the bed. His lips brushed her brow with a light good-night kiss. "Now, go to sleep."

Tyler lay down beside her, and moments later she heard the comforting sound of his soft, purring snore.

Choking back tears of disappointment and frustration, Gail lay awake far into the night, racking her brain for a way to keep Tyler from gallivanting off to the sunny climes of the South Seas.

 3

A DRAFT OF cool air brushing Gail's bare shoulder awakened her. Drowsily, she rolled over, seeking the comfort of Tyler's warm body. Startled, her eyes flew open. A cold, empty hollow remained in Tyler's place.

"Gone!" cried a voice in her head, as if he'd already abandoned her. "Tyler's gone!"

And then she heard the pipes groan, the sputter and hiss and the spurt of water that meant someone had turned on the faucet in the bathroom. She pictured Tyler standing before the mirror, brushing his strong white teeth. Or shaving, maybe, carefully scraping a soapy-white beard from high-planed cheek to sturdy jowl.

Reassured by the familiar sounds that meant he was home, Gail ran her hand over the depression in the mattress. This is the way it will be when Tyler goes away, she thought gloomily, a cold, lonely, empty bed. Her mind and heart rebelled, refusing to accept the possibility. She could not, would not, take him seriously. But he had said he was going, and Tyler Peabody was a man of his word. Still, she could not believe he was *really* going.

All last evening Tyler had played his stereo and said no more about giving up his job or running off to a desert island. Now she wondered uneasily if Tyler had spent the evening with her just to be kind, *because* he was leaving her.

Firmly, she told herself that the whole thing was a nightmare, a bad dream, from which she had now awakened. A bad dream from which Tyler would awaken, soon, she assured herself.

"But if he *does* go," the demon voice persisted inside her head, "what will you do without him?"

Her chin rose in a defiant tilt. She said aloud, "I can certainly survive as a single person. No doubt about that! But I don't *want* to do without him. I *won't* do without him!"

It came to her then that although Tyler had turned her world upside down, *his* world appeared to be as "business as usual." Normal as apple pie. She could hear the hollow tattoo of the shower beating down on his lanky, muscular body, could envision rivulets of water streaming down his taut limbs. And, as usual, she could hear him singing, loudly and slightly off key, "Some Enchanted Evening." This morning, his choice of tunes gave her an unpleasant turn.

She sat up in bed and gazed fixedly out the window. The view of the lush countryside, fields and meadows laced with low stone fences, and the steeple of the village church stretching heavenward, never failed to inspire her. The sun, shining with optimistic brilliance, highlighted crimson-hued maples and gilded the tips of dark, furry pines. A majestic white oak flaunted a leafy garnet canopy, and the distant hills, quilted in muted shades of green, gold, and scarlet, were seamed with the glistening silver thread of the river.

Inspiration dawned. She would fix Tyler's favorite cold-weather breakfast: fried eggs, sausage, blueberry pancakes, and apple pie. Surely he would be struck with the realization that no native maiden on his desert island would dish him up eggs, sausage, blueberry pancakes, or apple pie, and he'd better think twice before flying off to distant shores and climes.

Further inspired, instead of donning her usual sculpting outfit, blue jeans, T-shirt, and running shoes, she would slip into the long, clinging burgundy *panné* velvet robe Tyler had given her for her birthday. He had told her that the rich color enhanced her fine, lustrous skin, and wearing it, she reminded him of a Rembrandt portrait of his mistress, Saskia. The thought of looking like Saskia was now infinitely intriguing.

She smiled to herself, remembering how Tyler had pulled her to him, calling her his sensuous woman; how he had run loving, tender hands up and down the smooth, satiny velvet that clung to every soft curve, every peak and valley, of her figure.

And instead of capturing her long, wavy black hair in a barrette at the back of her neck, she would let it tumble over her shoulders and down her back, as she imagined native females on a desert island would do. She would go barefoot, as well. But the instant her feet hit the cold, polished pine floor, her Yankee practicality raised a hue and cry. Swiftly, she slid her slender feet into cozy fleece-lined leather moccasins. Standing before the full-length pier glass in the bedroom, she regarded her reflection doubtfully. Leather moccasins did nothing to enhance the glamorous image she had in mind.

With the combination of the clinging Rembrandt robe, and her hair flowing wantonly down her back, and a breakfast fit for a king, Gail hoped Tyler would decide he had the best of both worlds right here at home in Connecticut. With a wistful sigh, she reflected that Tyler had always been idealistic, a dreamer, qualities he attributed to the fully developed creative right side of his brain. But the efficient, reasoning, mathematical left side of his brain had developed equally well. Yes, Gail thought, encouraged, there was definite reason to believe Tyler would come to his senses.

Bursting with good intentions and good cheer, she padded down the back stairs into the kitchen. At the sight of her, Sidney leaped up from his wicker basket beside the fireplace, bounded about the room barking a greeting, then dashed to the back door. Gail opened the door for the dog. A soft, warm breeze bearing the winey fragrance of windfall apples wafted through the room. She could scarcely believe it after yesterday's cold snap, but here was summer sneaking through the door. Betrayed by the weather, she thought with a twinge of vexation, leaving the door ajar for Sidney. It was really too warm for Tyler's favorite cold-weather breakfast. Well, he was going to get the full treatment, Indian summer or not.

At the sound of Tyler's springy footsteps pounding down the stairs, she slipped off her moccasins and tossed them into Sidney's basket. Tyler, freshly shaven, reeking with Lagerfeld after-shave lotion, appeared in the doorway wearing a plaid shirt, a jacket, and slacks that he fondly referred to as his chocolate cords. Moving her hips in an undulating, seductive way, Gail crossed to greet him.

With an abstracted air, he planted a kiss on the tip of

her upturned nose. She gazed up into his face, her lips parted in an inviting smile.

Tyler's mild, questioning gaze traveled over the thick, glossy black hair curling around her shoulders, down the length of the burgundy robe molding her breasts, narrow waist, and softly rounded hips, to her bare toes. His sandy brows drew together in a scowl. "Good grief, Gail! Where are your shoes? You'll catch your death of cold."

Stung, she strode to Sidney's basket, slipped on her moccasins, then marched to the back door and slammed it in the face of the summery weather. She whirled to face Tyler, her eyes raking his chocolate-brown corduroy jacket and slacks. "And where is your gray flannel business suit—and your white shirt and your rep-striped tie? You can't go to work in that outfit!"

Grinning indulgently, Tyler bent down and kissed the dimple in her chin, then crossed to the counter and poured himself a cup of coffee. "I'm slaving at home today. It's Sunday, remember?"

Gail felt warmth steal into her cheeks. In her befuddled state, she'd forgotten. Determined to have the last word, she said, "Well, you're mighty dressed up for working at home."

His lips curved in an enigmatic smile. "When I finish working, I have an errand to run in the village." With no further explanation, he poured a cup of coffee for Gail and sat down at the gateleg table. "Umm, something smells good. What is it?"

She started to ask, "What's your errand?" Then, remembering that she was trying to make points with Tyler, she said lightly, "Warmed-over apple pie, darling." She set his plate on the table along with a pitcher of golden maple syrup, then filled her own plate and sat down across from him. She was dying to know what his errand was. Tyler abhorred running errands. If there was no escape, to make them less distasteful, he always asked her to ride along with him. With an effort, she curbed her curiosity and waited for him to ask.

Tyler said nothing. Gail said nothing. She could feel her dander rising like hackles on the back of her neck. She tossed her head in a defiant gesture. She would not pry. She let the silence stretch on, hoping he'd eventually explain his mysterious errand. But he set to, devouring his breakfast with gusto and declaring her to be the best cook in Connecticut. Perversely, she thought he *could* have been more gallant and said "the entire world."

Tyler finished the last of his pie, drained his coffee cup, and let out a groan—whether because he was stuffed, or because he had to work, Gail couldn't tell—then went into his study and closed the door.

Gail gritted her teeth and scowled down at her clinging velvet robe. Tyler was apparently impervious to glamour. She changed into jeans, a yellow T-shirt, and running shoes and returned to the kitchen. With renewed resolve, she flung meat, carrots, onions, and potatoes onto the butcher-block counter. Soon a beef stew was simmering in the kettle that hung on the old iron crane over the fire on the hearth. She turned her attention to her African violets on the sill and, with a vengeance, pinched off every innocent, dried-up head. That done, she attacked the windows, washing Sidney's noseprints from the glass with unusual vigor.

At noon, Tyler looking frazzled and bleary-eyed, stuck his head around the keeping-room door, sniffing the air like a hound dog scenting a coon. "What's for lunch?" he asked.

Still desperately hoping to reach his heart through his stomach, Gail served him a bowl of the savory stew that had been simmering all morning, along with some hot, crusty garlic bread, and a glass of hearty burgundy. Once again he ate ravenously, then retreated to his study without mentioning his errand.

In the afternoon Gail occupied herself and her thoughts sculpting in her light, airy, glassed-in studio over the enclosed back porch. Engrossed in modeling just the right curve between neck and shoulder of a nude nymph for Tyler's rose garden, she didn't hear him leave the house. But shortly before suppertime she heard the low throb of a motor and the familiar sound of tires crunching down the gravel lane. She ran to the window and saw Tyler behind the wheel of their old VW convertible, easing into the barn.

She stood watching for him to reappear, her nose pressed against the cold, small-paned glass. Her heart beat faster as he emerged from the barn, his tall, rangy figure swinging across the driveway, past the brown-leafed rosebushes he had laid out with geometric precision. A small, anguished pang of love twisted inside her. His loping, loose-jointed, devil-may-care stride was one of the things she loved about him. In his left hand, he clutched his brown leather attaché case. She shook her head, marveling. Tyler might have been born naked, like everyone else, but she'd bet he'd had an attaché case in his hand.

Dear, dedicated, diligent Tyler. She smiled ruefully, feeling foolish at being put out over his mysterious errand. Clearly, he had trekked off to the post office in the village to drop some highly important—they were always highly important—papers in the mail. Even during these days, which Tyler dreamed would be his last with Connecticut Liberty Life, he was working his head to the bone.

A worried frown creased her brow. He was working too hard. On that they agreed. Nevertheless, with the thought that Tyler could never leave his work, a feeling of calm reassurance flowed through her. The New England work ethic was deeply ingrained in him. He would have to cut back, learn to relax at home.

It wasn't until after dinner, when Gail curled up in the gold wing chair in the keeping room, that Tyler lowered the boom. She was sewing contentedly on a square of lap quilting. With deft, slender fingers, she wielded the flashing needle through the thick fabric, outlining a pink tulip with neat, tiny stitches.

Tyler strode into the room, attaché case in hand, a jubilant expression lighting up his face. He sank down in his Lincoln rocker across from her chair.

She looked up, her lips parted in a piquant smile. Her voice held a note of entreaty. "Tyler, surely you're not going to work tonight! It's Sunday, remember? Can't you take one night off?"

Smiling warmly, he balanced the attaché case on his knees and snapped open the shiny brass locks. His sherry-colored eyes sparkled with excitement. "I have something to show you." He flipped back the lid. Then, scooping up a handful of colorful brochures, he thrust them into her lap. "Look! Tahiti, Samoa, Pitcairn Island—take your pick."

Her fingers froze on her quilting hoop and needle. She gazed down at the bright collection of travel folders as though viewing a nest of snakes.

Exuberantly, Tyler went on, "I stopped by the travel agency this afternoon and talked with Miss Curtis..."

"On *Sunday!*"

"Right. She's new in this business. Eager to build up a clientele. Opens up on Sundays from one to five for the convenience of her customers—like me. She's fantastic! Says I don't have to book through one of the big Hartford agents. She can book me anywhere, anytime."

I'll bet! thought Gail, stabbing her shining shaft into the heart of the tulip.

"She's even put in for my passport and visa. She took my picture right on the spot and I filled out all the forms, so I should have them by the end of the month."

Dumbfounded, Gail withdrew her hands, which were deathly cold, from under the pile of brochures. "You— you can't," she stammered. In reality, she wanted to shout, "You can't go!" Instead, she said tightly, "You can't get a passport without your birth certificate."

Tyler cocked his head, staring at her in mild surprise. "Well, of course, darling. I took it with me."

"Of course," Gail echoed numbly. Her mind was reeling, and she felt a heavy sinking sensation in the pit of her stomach, as if she'd swallowed a stone. Tyler had not gone to the post office, he had gone to a travel agency. Through waves of shock, the truth bore in on her. He *really* means to leave, she thought dully. *Really* intends to go away from the village, from this house, from me, to some faraway place, for... forever?

He perched on the seat of the rocker and fished a brochure from Gail's lap. "Now, let me show you this."

The words TAHITI—PARADISE OF THE PACIFIC! leaped out at her. She scowled at a photo in glowing color of a smiling nut-brown girl—with a scarlet hibiscus tucked in her long, flowing hair—splashing in a turquoise sea.

"You have to help me decide where to go." He shook open the brochure, and spread the fanlike folds across her knees. "The capital is Papeete. That's much too commercial, too crowded. But there's a group of little islands not too far away that may still be deserted, unspoiled. When I say 'deserted,' I'm speaking relatively, you understand."

Gail stared numbly at the brochure, unable to relate to any of the dazzling tropical scenes.

Tyler, happily unaware of her utter dismay, pulled out another brochure. "Now, listen to this, about Samoa. There's Western and American Samoa: 'A group of fourteen islands in the South Pacific, only about forty-eight hundred miles southwest of San Francisco. Tutuila, in American Samoa, is the largest, fifty-four square miles.' Can you beat that—the entire island only fifty-four square miles? Pago Pago—Miss Curtis says it's pronounced 'Pango Pango'—is the capital." Tyler let out an ecstatic sigh. "All my life I've longed to see Pago Pago!"

Stunned, Gail wondered how on earth she could have lived with this man for seven years and never once heard him say that all his life he had longed to see Pago Pago. The cluster of microscopic dots on the map swirled before her eyes, merging into a blue blur. Still she said nothing.

Tyler went on, his voice rising in excitement. "Pago Pago, too, looks like a fairly substantial city. Miss Curtis thinks I may prefer to see Western Samoa."

Vengefully, Gail thought that *she* would prefer to see Miss Curtis roasting on a spit.

Tyler's long, sturdy forefinger jabbed the map enthusiastically. "The two largest islands in Western Samoa are Savaii and Upolu. Upolu, you probably recall, is where Robert Louis Stevenson lived for many years. As a matter of fact, he's buried there, on Mount Vaea, at the end of The Road of Loving Hearts." Glancing up at Gail as if for approval, Tyler gave a cheerful chuckle.

"And what's good enough for Robert Louis Stevenson is good enough for Tyler Phineas Peabody, right?"

A cold shiver ran up Gail's spine. The thought of Tyler buried at Robert Louis Stevenson's side did not cheer her. "Tyler! You can't mean that! You can't mean you'd become an expatriate, content to spend the rest of your life on foreign soil?"

He shrugged, smiling. "Who knows?"

With an effort, she said calmly, "I wouldn't count on staying forever, Tyler. Remember, your mother has already reserved both our graves in the Peabody family plot. Daphne would be very, *very* unhappy if your remains were to be buried in Upolu." Her throat constricted, but she forced herself to finish. "I'm sure you don't want to make Daphne unhappy...she's been so good to us."

For a moment, Tyler appeared nonplussed. Then his expression cleared. "You could always come over and get me."

Gail gave an emphatic shake of her head. "No way! Besides, I may get to heaven before you."

As if shot with an arrow, Tyler sat bolt upright in his Lincoln rocker. "Gail! How can you say such a thing? Don't even *think* it!"

Swiftly, Gail gathered up the brochures, dumped them on Tyler's lap, and rose from her chair. "I don't like to talk about these things, Tyler. It depresses me."

Crestfallen, he protested, "But I haven't told you about Pitcairn Island. That's where the mutineers from the *Bounty* were..."

Gail wasn't listening. With a shock of recognition, it came to her that until now, she hadn't, in her secret heart, taken Tyler seriously. She had simply been riding out this nor'easter in her husband's soul, sure that he would come to his senses. How could she have been so wrong? She would have to *do something*—but what?

A fine mist clouded her eyes, threatening to spill over and rain down her cheeks. Wordlessly, she picked up her quilting and fled from the room.

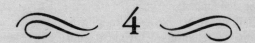

4

ON MONDAY, THE capricious September weather turned cold again. Gusting winds and slashing rain battered the windows and bowed the limbs of the majestic white oak, the gaudy maples, and the buttonwood trees.

Tyler, wearing a charcoal-gray suit, stood staring out the bedroom window, shoulders hunched, hands in his pockets, his mouth turned down at the corners, looking like a thundercloud. A heavy sigh escaped him.

Gail went to him and locked her arms about his waist, resting her cheek in the warm hollow between his shoulder blades. "Why so gloomy, darling? You look as though you'd just read your name in the *Doomsday Book*."

Tyler jerked his head toward the window, where needles of slanting rain fell in a fine gray screen. "It *looks* like doomsday."

Gail usually rose to greet the day with shining optimism. This morning, recalling the way their lovemaking had ended last night, she felt like yesterday's rose after a drenching rain. Resolutely, she banished her unpleasant thoughts and assumed a bright, cheerful air.

"I love these dark, dismal, dreary days. I feel so snug and safe and cozy inside with a fire roaring in the fire-place, and with Sidney stretched out on the floor guarding the home and something good baking in the oven."

He covered her hands with his, his fingers tightening in a companionable squeeze. "That's because you're a nester—and because you don't have to go out in it," Tyler said amiably.

Gail shook her head. "Wrong! I *love* storms, *love* defying the elements." Trying to infuse him with her own enthusiasm, she went on. "Besides, it would be boring to have that same old ho-hum sunshine every day. That's what makes September so fascinating. It's full of surprises. One day it's warm and sunny, and the next, cold and blustery, with the promise of fall."

Tyler shook his head. "Not for me." He turned to face her. "I don't like storms and I don't like surprises." Gail started to say that he certainly hadn't minded surprising her! But Tyler went on, his eyes glowing in anticipation. "I can't get to those tropical islands of sun and sand and crystal-blue waters soon enough."

Gail's spirits drooped. A feeling of desperate urgency overtook her. She would heed the small, insistent voice babbling inside her head.

Last night before drifting off to sleep, she had fed the problem of Tyler into her subconscious. All night long, her subconscious had wrestled with it. This morning she had awakened with the strong conviction that what Tyler needed was a challenge, something to spark his interest, something new and exciting to do, to take his mind off desert islands in the South Seas. She knew what *she* must do. And what Tyler must do.

She saw him off in a gust of wind and rain. As soon as the door had closed behind him, she rummaged frantically through the catchall drawer in the kitchen. Eagerly, she pulled out a handful of booklets and brochures and spread them on the table. Mingled hope and excitement churned inside her as she scanned catalogues from several colleges some distance away, a brochure from the YMCA in town, and a schedule of night classes at the local high school. After a little time, a pleased smile curved her lips. She had found exactly what she was looking for. Something Tyler would find challenging, intriguing, and exciting, and would snap at like a trout at a fly.

That evening Gail greeted Tyler at the door, all smiles. With an effort, she bided her time, waiting until after dinner—after he'd scaled the mountain of paper work in his study—to break the news. At last, Rousseau in hand, he sank down in his Lincoln rocker to read.

"Tyler," Gail said with a studied, casual air, as if she were about to comment on the weather, "I've found something for you to do that you'll really enjoy."

"Hmm," Tyler said, without looking up from Rousseau. "I have enough to do, darling."

"But you need to prepare for your trip."

He looked up from his book, regarding her with a bright, expectant smile.

Gail smiled back. It occurred to her then that springing it on him cold would be too great a shock. First the warm-up, she told herself. The slow curve, then the fast ball.

"You'll need something to occupy your time in Tahiti. How about basket weaving? I've studied your travel folders, and that's what the natives do. Weave baskets. Or you could climb coconut palms and shake down the fruit.

Or maybe you'd rather cut sugarcane with a machete, help harvest the crop."

Tyler gave a snort. "No way." He returned to Rousseau.

Gail grinned. "That's what I thought. What about mountain climbing? I read that in American Samoa, mountain slopes dip down into fertile valleys. To enjoy the view of the vast panorama of the aquamarine seas and white sand beaches, you'll have to climb to the tops of the mountains."

Tyler raised his head from his book and shot her a stern look. "Any mountain climbing I do will be in a Jeep or on the back of a mule, thank you."

Gail gave him a benevolent smile. "That's what I figured. So I signed you up for a scuba-diving class."

"Scuba!" Tyler exploded. "Scuba! If you signed me up for anything, it should have been sailing."

Unruffled, Gail went on. "I considered sailing, but since we don't have a boat, it didn't seem practical. Besides, it's too cold for sailing lessons."

"And it's too cold for scuba lessons," Tyler said flatly.

Smiling, Gail shook her dark, glossy head. "Not at the indoor pool at the Y."

Tyler fixed her with an incredulous stare. His eyes, as hard and bright as jewels, glittered with rebellion.

Gail laughed. "Don't stare at me as if I'd asked you to cross the desert barefoot. This is a perfectly sensible thing to do. I wouldn't want you to miss out on any of the pleasures the South Seas have to offer, and this is one of them. I mean, how often do you have a chance to scuba dive in Connecticut? Besides, it's only one night a week. Classes will be over by November first—when you make your Great Escape."

Tyler snapped Rousseau shut on his finger. In tones

of mingled insult and outrage, he shouted, "Do you know who takes those lessons? Kids! That's who! I'm not going to be the only adult there making a fool of myself."

Gail nodded with sympathetic understanding. "Right. You *won't* be the only one. I signed up, too."

"You!" Tyler cried, aghast.

Her lips curved in an implacable smile. "They require that you have a diving buddy."

Tyler's voice took on the patient tone of one reasoning with a fractious child. "But, darling, you're afraid of heights—and depths."

"Not in the pool at the Y."

"No way! And that's final."

"But, Tyler, what's the point of going to the South Seas if you can't see the sea?" She picked up one of his travel folders, with which she had armed herself in case of just such a crisis, and waved it under his nose. "You haven't done your homework. It says here that magnificent coral reefs abound and the lagoons teem with a rainbow of rare and colorful tropical fish. You'll be very sorry if you don't prepare yourself to see them. You are an adventurous person, Tyler. You'd *love* exploring the mysteries of the underwater world and meeting strange and exotic fish eyeball to eyeball." A devilish gleam came into her eyes. "Remember, you said we must be all we *can* be. You owe it to yourself!"

Tyler continued to stare at her in long, thoughtful silence. At last he muttered, "I don't have a tank, or a wet suit—not even goggles or flippers."

Undaunted, Gail said, "It says here that you can rent equipment on the islands. And, besides, you won't need a wet suit in the warm, soothing waters of the South Seas."

Tyler inclined his chin in a lofty, independent tilt. "I

may not go to the South Seas. I may go to the Sahara, or Wyoming."

Gail looked him straight in the eye with a stern, admonishing gaze. "But, Tyler, you know what you always say: Be prepared."

"Yes," Tyler conceded ruefully. "I *do* always say that." After a few more moments of silent contemplation, he said in grudging tones, "Well, I suppose you're right. When do classes start?"

"Tomorrow night," Gail said with a jubilant grin. "First an hour of lecture, then two hours in the pool."

That night before she went to bed, Gail penciled in the date of each lesson in *The Old Farmer's Almanac* in the catchall drawer of the kitchen. *Eight weeks!* Her pulse raced. Thoughtfully, she tapped the pencil against perfect white teeth. Of course, she would never beg Tyler to stay home against his will. But she could do her utmost to guide his will in a new direction. Only eight weeks, she thought grimly, to win Tyler over, to convince him that he should stay at home, that life was good right here in their white Colonial clapboard house in Connecticut. But she must think positively.

With a sudden lift of heart, she told herself that Tyler would revel in his new skill, conquering the underwater world; that scuba diving would tone up her muscles and trim her down; that she would no longer feel like "yesterday's rose." She would be a more exciting, youthful person in every way. And, most important of all, diving was a pastime she and Tyler would share.

Reassured, confident, buoyed by a feeling of cheerful optimism, she went to bed. But all night long she pitched and tossed, her sleep invaded by exotic, exciting dreams: visions of Tyler and herself garbed in goggles, flippers, and sleek, black, skintight wet suits, with yellow life jackets and tanks bobbing on their backs, laughing, running hand in hand into a foam-crested surf. Whether they were cavorting in the Bahamas, Bermuda, Cancun, the Cayman Islands, or the Florida Keys, she couldn't tell. All she knew was that she and Tyler were deliriously happy together.

Tyler was right, Gail thought with a slight sense of shock. When they strolled into the Y the following night, the classroom was crowded with brawny young men and shapely, well-toned young girls. The instructor, Jim Shockey, a short, muscular young man with cheerful mien, a fuzzy blond mustache, and intense blue eyes, banged the desk with his fist to get their attention.

"I'm the best scuba-diving teacher around," he said, strutting across the room. "Now, I want you to think of the underwater world as Utopia."

Gail glanced at Tyler with a knowing lift of her brows and a companionable smirk that said, "I told you so."

"I'm *king!*" Shockey continued. "What I say is *law!*" Tyler scowled. "You listen, do what I tell you, and *you'll* be the best divers around. Now, what does S-C-U-B-A mean?"

Silence shrouded the room. Suddenly, to Gail's astonishment, Tyler blurted out, "Self-contained underwater breathing apparatus."

Shockey beamed his approval. Eagerly, he told them about the equipment and its functions. Gail was surprised to hear that divers wore masks, not goggles; and fins, not flippers.

"Next week you'll need a face mask, snorkel, fins, and a textbook," Shockey went on. "You'll have a written test every week. And remember this: The cardinal rule of diving is, *Never dive without a buddy!* Now, everybody to the locker rooms. Get into your suits and report to the pool for your swim test."

Gail had no doubt that she and Tyler could pass the swim test. After all, they had not sat around on the bay at Cape Cod for two weeks every summer waiting for the tide to come in.

Languid as a water lily, she floated for fifteen minutes—grateful for the buoyancy with which nature had endowed her. She treaded water for three minutes, hanging on to her composure whenever Shockey shouted at her to keep her head back. Her endurance never faltered . . . until the underwater test. Swimming underwater for forty-five feet seemed like forty-five miles. Bleary-eyed, churning through the chlorine-scented pool, she thought to herself: Why, oh why, did I ever think I could become an amphibian! She clenched her jaw and clamped her lips in a thin, determined line. I don't know, she answered herself silently. But I can, and I will, if it means keeping Tyler in Connecticut! Just when she thought she couldn't swim another inch, her hand struck the skimmer trough. She lunged for it and hung on. A blast from Shockey's whistle pierced her ears.

"Life-saving, everybody. Choose a buddy, get a good grip on him, and swim the length of the pool."

Tyler, his hair plastered flat to his head, bobbed up from the depths like a sea lion. He flung an arm about Gail's shoulders.

"This is more like it," she said, shaking water out of her ears and grinning up at Tyler.

"Right!" He pulled her close against his warm, wet body, with her back nestled flat against his chest. He flung an arm across her breasts, his hand gripping her shoulder. Then he grinned down at her and, with his free hand, gave her bottom a friendly pinch.

"Ouch!" Gail cried in a loud voice. "There are crabs in this water!"

"Quiet, woman, or I'll throw you to the sharks!"

A whistle blast sounded. "Go!" shouted Shockey.

Tyler struck out. With his free arm, he stroked smoothly, cleanly, through the clear blue water. With every kick, Gail's bottom bumped comfortably against his sinewy thighs and her legs brushed sensuously against his. As they bumped the far end of the pool, the whistle shrilled again.

"Change partners!" shouted Shockey.

Eagerly, Gail clutched Tyler to her bosom. Entering into the spirit of things, playing his role to the hilt, he flopped like a dying porpoise at her side.

"Tyler!" Gail cried, hugging his head to her bosom. "Quit that! You make me nervous."

Tyler lay limp in her arms. Without opening his eyes, he nuzzled the valley between her breasts. In weak tones, he murmured, "I'm a drowning man. Save me."

Gail gritted her teeth and dragged Tyler's inert body the length of the pool. Without warning, at the end of the lap, she let go her hold. Tyler sank like a rock.

"Sink or swim!" she exclaimed gleefully, scrambling up the ladder. Shaking and winded, she dropped onto the deck.

Shockey's whistle shrilled. "Everybody into the pool! Swim six laps around—all four sides! I don't start counting till everybody's in the water!"

"You're kidding!" Gail cried, forgetting that Shockey was *king*.

By the third lap around, at a slow, even crawl, Gail was sucking air from the bottom of her lungs. Tyler had long since thrashed past her, winking, his lips curled in a superior grin. She flipped onto her back to rest. Chlorine stung her eyes and halos danced around the lights overhead. Tyler overtook her again, flashing her an amused, patronizing smile, as if to say he knew she couldn't make it.

"Male chauvinist!" Gail hissed savagely. With renewed determination, she rolled onto her side. By sheer force of will, she coerced her arms to move. With a slow, laborious sidestroke, she floundered through the remaining laps. Blindly, she climbed the ladder. Tyler stood waiting anxiously, stretching out a helping hand. A relieved smile crossed his face. "It was your sidestroke that saved you," he said, grinning.

Gail gave a defiant toss of her head, showering him with droplets of water. She felt groggy and her knees wobbled as they joined the class, clustered around a beaming Shockey.

"Congratulations!" he shouted. "You all passed!"

Afterward, driving home beside Tyler, in the crisp, clear light of the Full Sturgeon Moon, Gail said grimly, "I'm not sure I have the stamina to survive this class."

Tyler reached over and patted her knee. "Don't worry. You're just out of shape. Shockey said we'll swim six laps every night before class to build up our endurance."

"Only *six?*" Gail asked, in a voice tinged with irony.

"Actually, he said six or twelve laps. You'll be fine. It's going to be great!"

Gail groaned, thinking to herself that the only good thing about this venture was that Tyler seemed to enjoy it.

The following week, after a lecture and movie on first aid, they learned techniques. Gail learned how easy it was to spit on the fogged-up glass to clear her mask; to dunk her fins so they'd slip on easily; and that one did not dash headlong into the water wearing fins, but backed in to avoid tripping, or, better still, slipped them on after entering the water.

The third week, Shockey brought in tanks and regulators. "We each don our own equipment," he announced, eyeing Gail dubiously.

She ignored the twinkle in Tyler's eye as he watched her hoist the yellow, seventy-two-pound tank waist-high and set it down with a thud, narrowly missing her left foot.

"Don't let anything happen to those tanks!" Shockey yelled.

Quickly, she mastered the trick of sitting down on the deck in front of her tank, slipping the canvas straps over her shoulders, and buckling the harness around her waist. Her first mistake was popping up too quickly from the floor of the pool.

Shockey bellowed, *"Exhale* on your way up—don't you know you can drown in three feet of water if you forget to exhale?"

A warm, embarrassed flush spread under Gail's mask. She nodded, then quickly sank beneath the cooling waters.

She left the pool feeling breathless and exhausted. Strangely, at the same time, she felt giddy and exhilarated. She told Tyler about this after they came home from class. They had changed into their warm things: Tyler into his royal-blue velour robe, which Gail insisted he keep handy in case of fire, since he slept in the nude; and Gail into her Saskia burgundy robe. They lay stretched out on the braided rug before a blazing fire, their heads propped comfortably on Sidney's broad, sturdy back. Sidney lay with his head resting on his paws while Gail and Tyler toasted their toes and sipped hot chocolate topped with marshmallows from thick brown pottery cups.

"I have this great new sensation, Tyler, just the opposite from swimming underwater. I'm floating on air!"

Tyler laughed. "Me, too. It's all that oxygen we've sucked in. A new kind of high. Makes you feel really light-headed."

Gail turned to look at him, her lips curved in a provocative smile. "And light*hearted*, too, Tyler?"

He draped an arm around her shoulders and gave her an affectionate hug.

She placed a hand on his knee. "Who'd ever think you'd become the Jacques Cousteau of Connecticut!" She leaned heavily on the word *Connecticut*, but if Tyler noticed, he gave no sign.

Swirling a marshmallow around in his cup, he grinned down at her. "And who'd ever think you'd become the Jacqueline Cousteau of the underwater world!"

Gail's hand traveled gently up and down the long, lean length of Tyler's royal-blue velour-covered leg. "I love scuba diving together. I love doing things with you, Tyler," she went on wistfully. "Sharing new experiences."

Tyler tipped his head back and took a long swig of hot chocolate. "New experiences make a man healthy, happy, and wise."

Gail's fine arched brows drew together in a frown. "Who said that, Tyler?"

"I did."

Gail slipped her hand inside his robe, smoothing the springy hair on his thighs. She looked up into his face, her lips parted in a piquant smile. "You're already healthy and wise, Tyler. Aren't you happy, as well?"

"Oh, sure," Tyler said affably. "But I'll be a damned sight happier when I stop working and start living the good life on a desert island."

The mantel clock began to strike. To Gail, it sounded as if its seemingly endless bong, bong, bong, were tolling the knell of doom. Her lip quivered. Swiftly, she drained the chocolate from her cup and set it down on the table beside J. Alfred Prufrock, an orange flash, circling inside his bowl. Sidney leaped to his feet. Gail's and Tyler's heads bumped on the braided rug. Sidney's plumed tail thumped against the floor. He eyed them meaningfully, glanced at the door and then back again, a hopeful gleam shining in his blue and brown eyes.

"He knows it's ten o'clock," Gail said, sighing. "How can I compete with a dog that keeps a schedule!"

Tyler glanced at his watch. "Yep. Time for Sid's airing." He got to his feet. "C'mon, Sid. I'll take you out. But we're going out front tonight. It's too muddy in the back." He strode into the hallway, Sid bounding and barking joyously at his heels.

Sidney, you traitorous beast! Gail thought vengefully. How can I coax Tyler into a romantic mood with you around!

Impulsively, she jumped up, switched off the lamps, and snatched the needlepoint pillow from Tyler's rocker. Ruthlessly, she plucked three shiny, blue-and-green-eyed peacock feathers from the tin milk can by the door and returned to the fireside. Moments later she heard Tyler's light, firm step, and his deep, lazy voice as he entered the room.

"Hey, what's happened to the lights?" His tone turned to one of shocked surprise. "Holy smoke! What happened to your *clothes?*"

Gail, with one arm folded under her head on the pillow, and one hand resting on her left thigh clutching a feather fan, lay stretched out in a provocative pose on her *panné* velvet robe. Firelight danced on her skin, creating glowing highlights and rich, dark shadows. She gazed up at Tyler through half-lidded eyes. An inviting smile curved her full, moist lips.

"What clothes?" she asked in a throaty whisper. She let the feathers fall and lifted a languid hand, beckoning Tyler closer. "Come here, darling."

Tyler's knees folded like paper. Before she could bat an eyelash, he was seated on the floor beside her, propped on one elbow, leaning over her.

His fine, sherry-colored eyes, alight with joy and wonder, suddenly glowed with the heat of desire. "Saskia, come to life!" he exclaimed. He reached out and, placing his palms on her cheeks, kissed her lips. The fullness of his mouth, so soft and tender, pressing on her own, stirred all her senses. His kiss deepened. His hands trailed slowly down her neck, caressing the soft curves of her shoulders and breasts, sweeping aside the concealing peacock feathers. With restrained passion, he caressed every rounded, enticing contour.

A thrill of excitement surged through her. The gentle, persistent pressure of Tyler's fingertips kneading, stroking each rosy tip to a peak of tormented desire, aroused her to fever pitch. She sensed that he was holding back, waiting for her ardor to mount, wanting to prolong these moments of sweet enchantment.

She took up the peacock feathers. Her hand stole around Tyler's neck, dusting his shoulders, trailing down the lean, muscular length of his back, circling lightly around his waist, across his flanks, down thigh and calf, teasing the backs of his knees. She felt a convulsive tremor course through his body, heard his quick intake of breath.

"Quit torturing me, you wanton woman!" he whispered huskily. He rose to his knees and, with one swift swoop, snatched the feathers from her hand and tossed them into the air. His lips curved in a loving smile. An expression of mingled adoration and anticipation glistened in his eyes as he bent his head, covering her body with kisses as light and tender as the feathers floating down around them.

Reveling in his kisses, Gail closed her eyes, giving herself over to the rapturous sensations tingling through her body. Never had Tyler been so romantic, so adoring. Ripples of delight flowed through her. He clasped her slender feet between his hands and brushed each arch, every pink-tipped toe, with quick, loving kisses. Without knowing she did so, Gail murmured her thoughts aloud. "Tyler Peabody, I love you. Oh, how I love you. I cannot count the ways!"

"Try!" Tyler whispered.

Gail smiled. "Well, let me think. I love you because you're suave and debonair."

"More!" Tyler whispered, kissing the palms of her hands.

"And I love you because of your worldly charm and brilliance."

"More!" His lips circled her navel slowly, sensuously, unhurriedly moving upward, circling her breasts, nibbling each earlobe.

Gail entwined her fingers in his thick russet hair and brought his head up, her lips brushing his. "And I love you because you're the best lover I've ever known."

"Let's keep it that way," Tyler said fervently, gazing deeply into her eyes. His own eyes were luminous and the intensity of his gaze electrified her. He flung off his robe and lowered his warm, glistening body over hers. As he parted her thighs, a voluptuous sensation crept through her like tiny wavelets, then rose like a tide, washing over her in a great wave, engulfing her, carrying her upward, over the crest, assuaging her exquisite torment at last.

She lay in his arms, her body joined to his, reveling in the sweet bliss of feeling as one with Tyler. The fire crackled on the hearth. The heady fragrance of applewood perfumed the air and firelight danced on the ceiling, flickered on their naked bodies. At length the fire burned low and a glowing crimson log on the hearth shattered with a burst of starry sparks.

Pure joy enveloped her. Her heart sang with the certainty that now Tyler would never leave her. She had never felt happier, more sure. She opened her eyes and looked up into his face. His lips were swollen with passion. His drowsy, loving gaze locked with hers. He reached out and smoothed a few damp, tousled curls back from her forehead. When at last he spoke, his voice was rough with emotion.

"The worst thing about going away is leaving you." He let out a long, hopeless, helpless sigh. "I'm going to miss you, my love." He closed his eyes, murmuring, "'To sleep, to sleep, perchance to dream.' Hamlet."

Gail's heart staggered. A sudden chill stippled her smooth flesh. The words "Then don't go, Tyler, please don't go!" trembled on her lips, but pride—her inborn New England Yankee pride—prickled like the quills of a porcupine held at bay. Never would she beg a man not to leave her! If he wanted to go, then begone, and good riddance!

She put her hands on his shoulders and gently rolled him aside. Wordlessly, she gathered her robe about her nude body, feeling as shattered as the glowing embers dying in the hearth. She slipped it on, clutching it tightly about her, as if for protection. Tyler lay prone on the braided rug, eyes closed, smiling in dreamy contentment. He was asleep! Softly, she said, "Good night, Tyler."

She climbed the stairs to their room and flung herself down on the bed. One minute she convinced herself that Tyler would stay, and the next minute he convinced her he was really going, leaving her feeling bereft and sick at heart. She closed her eyes, as if to shut out the vast, empty darkness. This is the way it will be after Tyler leaves, she thought. Cold and lonely and dark. She had never felt so miserable in her entire life. Tears rose in her throat. She choked them down and compressed her lips in a determined line. She would have to beef up her campaign to keep Tyler at home.

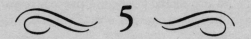 5

IF TYLER HAD the feeling that Gail was all but pushing him out the door, he was right. But this morning she didn't care. She could hardly wait to plan the next phase of her campaign. She poured herself another cup of coffee and sat down at the table to do some hard, solid thinking. The crux of the matter, she'd decided, was to get to the root of Tyler's problem. He'd admitted he'd been thinking for some time about making his Great Escape. But what had made him think of running off in the first place?

As if in a trance, she stared past the cheerful splash of pink, purple, and white African violets on the windowsill, trying to focus her thoughts. Gradually, a thought she had never before imagined surfaced. Like an old, bleached bone dislodged from the bottom of the sea during a violent storm, it bobbed to the surface of her mind. Shaken to the core, she exclaimed aloud, "Another woman!"

Sidney leaped from his basket, loped to her side, and put his head in her lap. Absently, she scratched his ears, turning the startling thought over in her mind. The words "another woman" echoed and re-echoed in her head. Tyler? Impossible! Plainly, her mind was going. She was no longer rational. This was a matter a woman could talk over only with her best friend. She fixed her fond gaze on Sidney.

"Sidney, sit. Now, don't you agree that Tyler latching on to another woman is impossible?"

Sidney raised his eyes to hers. Through his black-spectacled white mask, he regarded her with a quizzical, soulful expression, as if to say, "Sad, but possible."

His grave, unrelenting gaze made her uneasy. Now that she thought of it, why was it so impossible that Tyler had found another woman? A devastating thought squeezed her heart. Even if Tyler hadn't found some other woman, maybe some other woman had found him! He was warm, responsive, lovable, full of boyish charm, fun to be with, desirable. Why wouldn't another woman find him as irresistible as she did?

Morosely, Gail went on, "It all fits, Sidney. Tyler never showed any signs of unrest and rebellion before his promotion to the home office. This wild yearning to be free must have been growing in his heart all along, and we never noticed because he was gone from Monday to Friday." Another, more devastating, thought struck that made her sit bolt upright, ramrod-stiff in her chair. Had Tyler found female companionship during the long, lonely evenings in motel cocktail lounges when he was on the road?

Gail stopped scratching Sidney's ears. Her fingers curled, nails biting into her palms, as she conjured up a vision of a dimly lighted lounge, and small, round tables graced by lovely, lonely traveling salesladies with come-hither looks in their eyes, their long, crossed, nylon-clad legs swinging seductively in time to soft, romantic music. She envisioned their intimate glances, the invitation in their eyes, their smiling lips, a dime-sized dance floor where everyone danced cheek to jowl, hip to hip.

Sidney thrust his damp black nose under Gail's curled fingers. She stroked his head consolingly.

"You can see how easy it would be, Sidney, to strike up a little conversation with someone, especially if she sat down at your table. And an innocent chat could turn into an..." She struggled to find a word less painful than "affair." She finally came up with the term "a relationship." She let out a long sigh. "Poor Tyler. Never met a stranger, and wouldn't hurt a woman's feelings for the world. Striking up an acquaintance with him would be like shooting fish in a barrel."

Now, of course, he wasn't on the road, but there were still scores of lonely ladies—secretaries, salespersons, executives—at Liberty Life, longing for someone to dote on, to dote on them. Spinsters left on the shelf, divorcées, widows, all oozing with life and vigor, missing male companionship, seeking solace, romance. Her imagination took flight. Some would be quiet and shy; others would be like piranhas, looking for a good time, exciting to know, efficient, outgoing, immaculate, wearing beautiful clothes and getting weekly hairdos. Not free spirits like herself, in old jeans or leotards, without even an intention of exercising.

Frantically, she searched through her memory trying to recall whether Tyler had mentioned anyone special at the office. She could remember only one woman, Mary Embry, a sweet, plump, fifty-two-year-old widow with four kids to see through high school and college. If Tyler had succumbed to another woman's charms, he'd never spoken her name.

She slipped a hand under Sidney's chin and brought his head up to gaze directly into his earnest blue and brown eyes. "They say every dog has his day. Is this true, Sid?" Sidney stared solemnly back at her. "Tyler is no dog, but he's definitely acting as if he's having his day. Still, our dear, darling Tyler isn't exactly a wolf, either."

Or is he? she wondered. Lately he'd surprised her, wanting to quit his job to make the Great Escape, seducing her in the sunlit afternoon. She breathed a hopeless sigh. Did one person ever really *know* another?

"What do wives do at times like these, Sidney? I, for one, absolutely refuse to cop out!" At the word *out*, Sidney perked up his ears, wagged his tail vigorously, and strode to the door. Ignoring him, Gail murmured, "I know one thing, Sid. Wives are always the last to know, unless they have a well-meaning friend to tell them the news."

She had friends, of course, but no bosom buddy to bring her bad tidings. For a fleeting moment, she was sorry she was such a lone wolf. Then a steely gleam of determination lighted her eyes.

"Action, Sidney! That's the answer. Bless Bess if I'll sit around doing nothing while some strange predatory female destroys my marriage and ruins my life!"

Abruptly, she rose from the table and fished out the phone book from a drawer. Quickly, she flipped through the Yellow Pages. "I know one thing wives do in this sort of crisis. They hire someone to find out what's going on!"

Her heart beat fast with nervous excitement. What heading did shadowing a husband come under? DETEC-

TIVE? INVESTIGATOR? PRIVATE EYE? SPY? UNDERCOVER
AGENT? She started with the D's.

She ran a nervous finger down the page past DESIGN-
ERS—INDUSTRIAL, and DESK PADS & ACCESSORIES. There
it was: DETECTIVE AGENCIES! "Good grief, Sidney, there's
a whole raft of them! ACE's ace-of-spades logo looks
too menacing." She scowled, envisioning a short, squat
man with a blue stubble on his chin, a slouch hat pulled
low over his eyes, and a rumpled trenchcoat, dogging
Tyler's every step.

"ACE gives a confidential free consultation; divorce
evidence secured. We don't want a divorce, do we, Sidney?" Sidney gave a short, sharp bark. "ACE also finds
missing persons. But Tyler isn't missing yet—at least
not physically, only in heart and mind," she added dolefully.

Gail frowned down at the page. "And there's ACME,
surveillance and undercover investigation. 'Undercover'
sounds as if they leap into bed with the suspect. ALL
STAR offers polygraph tests—I doubt Tyler would take
kindly to that—and unfaithful spouse divorce investigations." Her lips thinned in a disapproving line. "Tyler
has given us no reason to believe he's unfaithful. I can't—
I *won't* believe it! He may be a little frisky, flirt a little,
tasting his freedom, but unfaithful? Never!"

Her finger moved on to BUREAU OF INVESTIGATION,
with a logo of a wide-open, all-seeing eye. "If only you
were a seeing-eye dog, Sid, you could be really useful."
Sidney gave an impatient whimper. Eagerly, Gail went
on. "Investigations of internal affairs. Nothing about *ex-
ternal* affairs. Suspicions verified." She gave an excla-
mation of distaste. "It all sounds so sinister, so sordid."
She slammed the book shut and thrust it back in the
drawer. "Enough of this maudlin talk." Sidney gave a

sympathetic whine. Gail crossed to the back door and flung it wide open, and as Sidney dashed through the doorway, she muttered to herself, "Good grief, even the dog wants out!"

As a matter of fact, the whole idea of hiring a detective to shadow Tyler was repugnant to her. She thought of shadowing him herself. But skulking around Liberty Life, hanging around till noon to see with whom he went to lunch, was just too demeaning. It smacked of sneakiness, which she abhorred. Of course, if he took some *femme fatale* to lunch, she would simply march right up to their table and join them. She would enjoy a nice lunch in a nice restaurant. But she hated that train ride to Hartford. And, besides, it would take a horrendous chunk of her time to trail Tyler all over the place. The plan just wasn't practical.

Another reason the idea of spying on Tyler herself was even more distasteful to her than hiring a detective was that she loathed the role of suspicious wife. She wouldn't, couldn't, play it. Worst of all, spying on Tyler would be a gross insult to his integrity. She would have to think of some other way to keep him from going off to a desert island.

By the time Tyler came home that night, looking tired and strained and careworn, Gail had thought of a new stratagem.

After dinner, as Tyler started toward his office, she put a hand on his arm and, smiling her most appealing, piquant smile, gazed up into his face.

"Hold on, my love. I have a special request."

Tyler, looking mildly astonished and curious at the same time, put his hands on her shoulders, grinning down at her. "Speak, my love. I'll give you the moon, the stars . . ."

"That's lovely, darling. But all I ask is a few minutes of your time. Just park your body in the rocker."

Tyler lowered his lean, lanky frame into his Lincoln rocker. He leaned his head back, looking utterly content. A faint smile curved his lips.

Gail sat down in the armchair across from him and took up a sketch pad and number-two pencil. "Perfect! Now stay put for twenty minutes." With quick, sure strokes, she began to sketch.

Pleased surprise glistened in Tyler's eyes. "I'm flattered no end, but when did you start doing portraits?"

"I haven't. This is just a sketch."

"Wouldn't you rather have a photograph? I mean, I could sit for a Bachrach in living color—save you a lot of time."

Her voice cracked a little. "I'll have nothing *but* time after you take off, Tyler. And, before you go, I want to sculpt a bust of you. I need a few preliminary sketches. Turn your head a bit to the left, love."

Tyler jerked erect in his rocker. "But, Gail, you take weeks, sometimes months, to sculpt a bust. You won't have time!"

"Yes, I will, Tyler, because after you quit Connecticut Liberty Life, you'll need a while to get ready to go."

"But, Gail, *I* won't have time!"

Tears welled in her eyes. She set down her pencil and gazed at him imploringly. "Tyler, please! I need a bust of you to make it through the lonely days and nights. Sculpting someone I know will go much quicker than sculpting a stranger. And suppose you never come back? It's *all* I'll have. And, besides, maybe the village fathers will want to mount a bust of you in the town hall or the library—a sort of memorial. All important men have busts made of them. Lincoln and . . ."

Tyler's face flushed crimson. Modestly, he lowered his gaze. "I'm not *that* important!"

"You are to me."

He smiled indulgently. "Well, I'll just have to make time to sit for you after I leave Liberty Life. And, as you say, it will go much quicker than if you were sculpting a total stranger..." He paused, staring thoughtfully at the ceiling.

Ruminating again, Gail thought savagely, thinking that lately *he* had acted like a total stranger.

"And, really," Tyler went on in magnanimous tones, "I guess I owe it to you—to leave you a memento of myself."

"Owe it to me!" Gail cried, incensed. "I'd have thought you'd *want* to leave me a memento of yourself!"

"Oh, I do! I promise you, darling. I do!"

An unlovely thought flashed into her mind. Was there someone *else* to whom he was leaving a memento of himself? Her imagination fired off another jolting thought. Maybe he was being driven to leave to escape an intolerable affair.

She had to *know*. And she'd be darned if she'd fish through his pockets and billfold searching for phone numbers or receipts, or scrutinize his shirts and handkerchiefs for telltale smears of lipstick. She couldn't bring herself to be so tawdry, so cloddish! She gazed directly into his eyes and, taking a deep breath, blurted straight out, "Tyler, is there another woman in your life? Have you fallen in love with someone else?"

Tyler's russet brows flew up. His warm brown eyes bulged. His mouth fell open. Total, absolute shock made him look as if he'd been hit by a high-tension wire of ten thousand volts.

"Gail! Are you out of your mind?"

She felt a great flood of relief sweep through her. His reaction had told her all she needed to know. But she wanted to hear him say it. She kept her level gaze on his face. Her voice trembled. "Just about."

Tyler jumped up from the rocker. In three great strides, he crossed the room, scooped her up in his arms, and sank down in the armchair, cuddling her close against his chest. He pressed his cheek against hers, speaking in choked, husky tones. "I shouldn't even need to say it, Gail, but I swear, there's no other woman, never has been, never will be."

Gail summoned a smile. Tyler was the soul of integrity. If he said there was no other woman, there wasn't.

"I believe you, Tyler." As if to reassure him, she added, "And there's no one else for me, either."

A startled expression sprang to his eyes. "I never for one instant thought there was."

He placed a hand under her chin, tilting her face up to his. He kissed the tears from her eyelids and his lips claimed hers in a long, deep kiss. But after some little time, her mind began to function again. Reason reasserted itself, overriding her feeling of relief. Abruptly, she slipped from Tyler's warm, sheltering arms and sat stiffly upright on his knee, looking like a thundercloud.

Taken by surprise, Tyler said with an injured air, "What's wrong? Why the about-face?"

A troubled expression came into her eyes. "Tyler, if you're not leaving me for another woman—and I know you aren't—it means you're leaving me for no earthly reason. Your leaving is bad enough, but leaving for no earthly reason is adding insult to injury!"

His expression turned pleading. "Gail, can't you simply take what I say at face value? I'm fed up with being what other people—parents, teachers, bosses—have been telling me all my life that I should be. I'm going because it's a thing I have to do. I'm going to find myself, to find *me!*"

Feeling utterly miserable, Gail shook her head. "I feel as though I've been swept out to sea with neither charts nor compass—in a rowboat with no oars. I've failed you, Tyler. But how?"

Tyler threw up his hands in a hopeless, impatient gesture, then slapped them down on the arms of the chair. "That's ridiculous."

His annoyance fired her own. Like an express train hurtling down a fast track, she rushed on: "All these years you've misled me, Tyler. I should have insisted on giving those intimate little dinners you always said you loathed. I should have held cookouts with our neighbors, urged you to buy a sailboat and join the yacht club like other couples we know. I should have built a swimming pool over your howling protests at every scoop of earth dug from your precious garden. I should have entered into the social life you claimed you detested, and refused to believe you when you said all you wanted when you came home from fighting the corporate battle all week was to relax in your rocker, chew on your pipe, listen to the stereo, and read Rousseau."

Tyler reached up and smoothed her dark, curly hair back from her fevered brow. "Hey, wait a minute. To me, you've always been Mrs. Wonderful. You're all mixed up..."

"No, Tyler. *You're* mixed up, or you wouldn't be leaving. You never should have married me. I'm a very private person, a loner. All wrong for you. I should have dived into the swim of things so we'd both have a place in the life of the village. That our marriage has come to such a pass is all my fault!" A sudden shower of tears rained down her cheeks, and try as she would, she couldn't stop them.

Tyler yanked his monogrammed linen handkerchief, which he normally never used, from his breast pocket and gently mopped the tears from Gail's face.

"Now, now, my love, listen to me. My decision to leave home has nothing to do with you, is no reflection on you, nothing personal."

Unconvinced, Gail sniffed loudly.

In tones of earnest confession, he went on: "The truth is, I never should have married *anyone*. I should have been a monk. A hermit living in a cave. I've finally realized that our marriage isn't fair to you. I've even deprived you of having children."

Gail cried out in protest. "Now, Tyler, I won't let you take the blame for that. It's not your fault that you had an adulthood bout with mumps. Besides, we may not be deprived. After all, the adoption agency has *promised* us a child. Ours could be born tomorrow, or next month. And," she went on sadly, "if it is, you won't be here . . ."

"Promises, promises," Tyler chanted. "They've been *promising* us for three years!" He gave an exasperated shake of his head. "There are too many birth-control devices and too few mothers giving kids away. You can't count on anything these days."

"Tyler, darling," Gail said fervently, "I'd rather have you than *ten* children."

"I understand," Tyler agreed soberly. "But you must understand that for years I fought the battle of a young man on his way up the corporate ladder. Now, I've arrived. What else is there? I'm sorry, darling, but I must find my true niche in this world. You are one of the lucky few who have already found their calling—you've found your niche as a sculptor. And," he ended on a triumphant note, "you found it in Italy!"

"Tyler, that was only a three-week art tour, four years ago."

"Still, you found your niche in Italy, not Connecticut."

Privately, Gail agreed that she had found her niche, but she never would be happy without Tyler to share it. Then and there, she resolved that he *would* share it.

"But, Tyler, how do you know your true niche is in Pago Pago or Samoa or Tahiti? How do you know it isn't right here in Connecticut?"

"I've looked in Connecticut. I haven't found it. I need a challenge." His eyes lighted with anticipation and determination, as if suddenly beholding the Holy Grail. "Tahiti offers a challenge, the opportunity to live free, a child of nature, Rousseau's natural man."

"But you love people, Tyler. Won't you be lonesome living on a desert island?"

"It may be a desert, but I don't believe it will be entirely *deserted*. I'm sure I can find someone to talk to if I feel lonesome, my love. You see, it's the *freedom* I need. Freedom to be me."

Gail nodded, trying hard to understand. Sympathy shone from her soft gray eyes. "It must be terrible not to be able to find yourself, Tyler."

He patted her hand, as if to console her, and himself as well. "You must try not to worry about me, love. I'll be fine. All things come to those who wait."

A broad smile curved Gail's full, generous lips. "I hope so, darling. I truly hope so!"

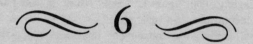

6

GAIL AWOKE THE next morning to a blaze of bright sunlight and the tangy fragrance of crisp autumn air blowing in the window. The fresh new day made her feel invigorated, swept the cobwebs from her mind. Her subconscious had labored hard throughout the long, dark night, and now her lips curved in a small, secret smile. She threw back the covers and bounded out of bed, fired with a new sense of purpose. The time had come to call out the reserve troops.

Scarcely able to contain her excitement, she gave Tyler his breakfast and a vitamin pill and sent him off to work with a kiss and a smile. She stood at the window, watching to be sure he wouldn't return for something he'd forgotten, that he was really on his way. At last she saw the old red VW chug down the lane. Swiftly, she brought out a pen and a box of stationery and sat down at the kitchen table.

She stared at her African violets, thinking hard. She must compose a letter that would fire up Tyler's mother,

the last grand matriarch of the Peabody family line.
Daphne loved a battle, and a set-to with her son would
fill her with delight. Although Daphne treasured her independence and preferred to lead her own gadabout life
in Phoenix, it had become a family tradition for her to
visit Gail and Tyler at Christmastime. All Gail needed
to do, she thought, was persuade Daphne to come a bit
earlier than usual.

Eagerly, Gail began to write. Warming to her task,
she recounted in great detail all the events of the past
month. Swept away by emotion, she swiped impatiently
at unbidden tears that stung her eyelids and sniffed loudly.
She told Daphne about her various attempts to prevent
Tyler from leaving, her ploys to make him change his
mind, all of which had fallen on deaf ears and a stubborn
mind. She ended with her fears for his health and safety.
Just pouring her heart out to Daphne made her feel much
better about the whole thing.

When at last she finished, she read the letter over,
slowly and carefully. She let out a long, dispirited sigh.
It sounded like the ravings of a hysterical, overimagi-
native wife. It was much too emotional, and too incredible to be taken seriously by a woman who knew what
was what, a staunch New Englander who was totally
rational and straight-thinking, not given to flights of fancy.
Daphne would think her daughter-in-law had gone off
the deep end, that she was making a mountain out of a
molehill, that *she* was the one living in fantasyland. Resolutely, Gail tore up the letter and took out a fresh sheet
of paper.

She must stick to the facts, and only the facts. After
much thought and consideration, she wrote a brief note
stating that in mid-November Tyler was quitting his job
and shortly thereafter was taking off to live on a desert

island. Deliberately, she omitted Wyoming and the Sahara, thinking they only made her story sound all the more fantastic. Smiling to herself, she ended with what she considered a masterstroke, giving the letter a truly personal touch. Tactfully, she pointed out that Daphne was about to lose her only son and child to the golden-brown-skinned natives of Tahiti, and if she ever wanted to see him again, she had better fly to Connecticut on the next plane from Phoenix.

A slight frown of concern creased her brow. Daphne never flew. She insisted it was because planes were so unreliable. Actually, she was terrified of flying, but the word "fear" was not in Daphne's vocabulary. Surely, the threat of losing Tyler would be enough of an emergency to make her take to the skies. But, whether she flew through the air, or took to the highway, Gail hadn't a doubt in the world that Daphne would heed her call to arms! In an optimistic mood, Gail sealed the letter, murmuring a desperate prayer that Daphne would arrive in time to save Tyler from himself.

Rationalizing that silence was golden, and discretion the better part of valor, Gail decided not to mention the letter to Tyler. If Daphne came, it would be a lovely surprise. If she didn't, well, then Tyler wouldn't be disappointed. She pushed back her chair and got up to take a look at *The Old Farmer's Almanac*.

As she spread the thick yellow booklet open on the counter, the pages fell open to November sixteenth. Clearly, it had been flattened many times at this particular page. Scowling, Gail tapped the pen against gleaming, even white teeth. There, in inch-high scarlet letters, Tyler had scrawled "GE" to mark the day of his Great Escape from the corporate rat race. As if either of us could forget! Gail thought gloomily. Of course, Tyler would need time to get ready before leaving for his desert island, but Gail knew that would only be a matter of a few days...

She flipped back to September, where she'd crossed off the date of each scuba lesson they'd taken. Now, all too soon, it was the twenty-eighth. Her optimism dissolved. Her spirits plummeted to her toes. Only five more scuba lessons. Less than two months till Tyler took off! There was no time to lose.

She grabbed up the letter, whistled to Sidney, and went outside. With Sidney cavorting at her heels, she scuffed through crisp fallen leaves to their mailbox at the end of the lane. She stuck the letter inside for the postman to pick up on his rounds. As she snapped the box shut, a marvelous feeling of accomplishment swept through her.

As if sensing her elation, Sidney was barking and jumping around in circles, clearly itching to set off on a hike. Gail longed to run with him down the long, sloping meadow behind their house, romp through goldenrod, scarlet Indian pipe, and Queen Anne's lace, play tag with him in the golden sunshine. Reluctantly, she shook her head. "Sorry, Sid. I have more important things to do, and no time to spare."

Minutes later she was seated before her easel gazing at Tyler's clay bust. Depression settled on her shoulders like a sparrowhawk as it bore into her that sculpting Tyler's bust was self-defeating. Suddenly, she felt torn asunder.

"I'm damned if I do, and damned if I don't," she muttered. "If I *don't* finish you, Tyler, I won't even have your bust to talk to. And if I *do* finish you, you'll feel free to go! I'm signing my own desertion warrant. But I'm not giving up, Tyler. Not on your life!" With renewed determination, she took up a tool. Gently, lovingly, she carved a smile on Tyler's full, generous mouth.

As the golden weeks of October flew past with breath-taking swiftness, Gail sculpted with ever-decreasing speed in a desultory way. What discouraged her further was that there had been no word from Daphne. Gail had tried several times to call her, but there was no answer. If Daphne had been any other woman, Gail would have worried about her. But Daphne was such a gadabout that finding her at home was simply a matter of luck. Gail would have to keep calling.

As the bright, brisk, blue October days wore on, Gail and Tyler's scuba-diving lessons progressed beyond her wildest expectations. As she had hoped, diving proved to be a new and exciting challenge to Tyler. With each lesson, he grew more enthusiastic. Gail crossed off the weeks in *The Old Farmer's Almanac* with increasing hope and optimism.

Tyler loved practicing "entries" from the diving board. Gail hated "entries." Inevitably, she somersaulted to the bottom of the pool, and millions of tiny stinging bubbles rose in her head. It was like sniffing champagne. She began to feel like J. Alfred Prufrock. But it was worth it, she told herself, to dive with Tyler.

Next they learned skills to avert panic. Gail was eager to learn how to avoid panic. Now, *there* was something really worth knowing. Panic, Shockey assured them, was the cause of most diving deaths. They would dive to the floor of the pool, doff their equipment and surface, then dive down again and don their equipment underwater. Gail felt less reassured when they practiced buddy breath-ing, just in case their air ran out, or their hose was bitten off by a passing shark.

That night, riding home beside Tyler through the tangy

fall darkness, Gail remarked, "Tyler, there's one thing I don't understand about buddy breathing. Why is it that when I hand you my regulator to take two breaths, you take forever to give it back? But when you hand it to me, I barely have time to inhale one deep, glorious whiff before you grab it back again!"

"Easy," Tyler said authoritatively. "I have bigger lungs and"—he patted her softly curving bosom under her T-shirt—"broader chest expansion."

Laughing, Gail grabbed his hand and brought it to her lips as if to bite it, but before she could sink her teeth into the heel of his hand, Tyler snatched it away.

With a lofty tilt of his head, he went on: "But as I always say, 'Quality counts more than quantity.' And, sweetie, you're quality!"

In tones of mock reproof, Gail said, "Will the driver please keep both hands on the wheel while he's handing out compliments?"

"Right on," Tyler said. Staring down the road with fierce intensity, he drove homeward.

Gail spent the next day doing one of her favorite things: taking a group of schoolchildren on a tour of the zoo. She got home late and hurried inside to start dinner without checking the mailbox at the end of the lane. It was Tyler who brought in the mail. Laughing, shaking his head in helpless admiration, he waved a picture post-card under Gail's nose. "That mother of mine must have been born with itchy feet, and wings on her heels!"

Gail's heart soared. *Daphne's on her way!* she thought, elated. Tyler's mother must be creeping toward Connecticut in her little Mercedes-Benz convertible! Eagerly, she snatched the postcard from Tyler's outstretched hand. On the back, in Daphne's firm, precise script, she read:

Having a fantastic time. Wish you were here!
All my love,
Daphne

Frantically, Gail flipped the card over. On the front
was a photograph of the Pyramid of the Dwarf, deep in
the heart of the dark green jungles of Uxmal, Mexico.
Gail felt as though a knife had pierced her heart. She
closed her eyes, blotting the card from sight. Clenching
her teeth, she said nothing.

On the following Wednesday, Gail stood at the kitchen
counter staring down at *The Old Farmer's Almanac*.
With an aching heart, she crossed off October twenty-
third. Last night the scuba class had practiced for its final
test next Tuesday. Tyler had all the skills down to a fare-
thee-well, and Shockey had pronounced him an expert
diver. At that, Tyler had wrapped his arms around Gail,
giving her a great bear hug.

"Darling, thank heaven you signed me up for scuba!
I no longer have any desire to go to the Sahara, not even
to Wyoming, which is a helluva lot closer..."

"Tyler!" Gail shrieked. In an excess of joy, she flung
her arms about his neck. "You've made me so happy!"

Jubilantly, he went on: "I've definitely decided to sail
to Tahiti!"

"But, Tyler!" Gail wailed, panicking, saying the first
thing that came into her head. "You don't know how to
sail!"

Tyler swept an arm through the air in a broad gesture.
"Figuratively speaking, my love. I'll sail through the
skies like an uncaged eagle to the 'Island of dreams, full
of peace and joy.' Melville."

Gail stiffened. Her fine gray eyes turned flinty. Hot
color rose in her face, creeping up to her hairline. She

stood stock-still, seething inside, glaring at her husband's smiling, exuberant face. With an effort, she bit back the words trembling on her lips: *That I'd like to see, because I'm going to clip the wings of the eagle.*

All the way home from the Y, Tyler had raved on and on about the delights of diving, and thanked Gail again for enrolling him in the class. If he was aware of her ominous silence, he gave no sign. Just thinking about last night made her blood boil.

The next morning she was ready to start clipping the wings of her freedom-loving eagle. Her eyes sparkled with purpose. Her full pink lips curved in a secret smile. She picked up the phone and called the florist.

Wednesday and Thursday passed with deceptive calm. The only clue that might have tipped off Tyler that all was not as it seemed was that Gail asked him not to go into the glassed-in sunroom at the back of the house. Every evening before Tyler came home, Gail drew the flowered draperies across the French doors opening onto the sunroom. Even this did not arouse his suspicions, for darkness came early now, and he well knew her compulsive urge to shut out the black night. If he had been more observant, thought Gail, relishing her secret, he might have noticed a mysterious, quiet, waiting quality in his woman. But Tyler, floating on a cloud of euphoria, as if he'd already taken to the skies, noticed nothing.

On Friday evening when Tyler came home from work, Gail, peeking from behind a drapery in the sunroom, watched him stride to the back door, whistling merrily, then halt dead in his tracks in the doorway. The whistle died on his lips. Clearly, he was flabbergasted that she wasn't there to greet him. She was *always* there to greet him. But not tonight. Nor was the table set. Nor were there any pots or pans bubbling on the stove, nor the yeasty aroma of bread baking in the oven.

"Gail?" She heard his voice rising on a note of panic. "Gail! Where are you?"

Gail called out in a cheerful, musical voice, "In the sunroom, darling. Come join me!"

She heard Tyler's light, quick steps crossing the polished pine floors. Suddenly the French doors were flung wide open. Tyler, who was never at a loss for words, stood on the threshold, stunned beyond speech.

With a small stab of satisfaction, Gail thought he couldn't have looked more astonished if a spaceship had landed in his rose garden and a Martian were rocking in his Lincoln rocker. With a languorous gesture, she flung her black, silken mane of hair over her shoulders and smiled invitingly. Proudly, she gazed about the room, seeing it as he must see it, transformed into a South Seas island paradise.

Huge potted palm trees banked the walls. Long, curling vines dangled from the ceiling. Scarlet and yellow hibiscus bloomed in each corner. In the center of the room, wooden bowls containing strange concoctions of food were spread on a coconut-frond mat on the floor. And, on the grill, now set indoors, a hefty suckling pig roasted on the spit. Soft, seductive ukelele music flowed throughout the room. Concealed lights shed a golden ambiance over all.

Gail's gaze zeroed in on Tyler, who stood as though mesmerized. His glazed eyes took everything in, coming to rest on his tan-skinned wife, clad only in a short skirt made of countless long, thin strips of hibiscus bark, and a red, black, and white feathered bandeau. She saw an expression of mingled shock and fascination suffuse his features as his dazzled eyes traveled to her bare feet, then up again to the crimson hibiscus tucked behind her ear. Her wavy, glossy black hair was tumbling down her back in wild abandon.

Before he could speak, Gail rose gracefully to her feet, walking with the supple, swaying motion of a young palm tree. Her lips curved in a ravishing smile as she handed Tyler a swatch of green, white, and yellow flowered fabric.

Suddenly regaining the power of speech, he bellowed, "What the hell is this?"

Undaunted, Gail said sweetly, "This is your lavalava." She thrust it into his hands.

"My *what?*"

"Your lavalava," Gail repeated patiently. "It's what all the men wear on Samoa."

"I'm going to Tahiti."

Gail shrugged. "Tahiti, Samoa. It's all the same," she said cheerfully. "Put it on, Tyler."

Tyler held the lavalava out before him at arm's length, viewing it as he would a dead rat. Indignation glittered in his eyes. "It looks like a wraparound skirt."

"Put it on," Gail said softly, "before we eat." Eagerly, she gestured toward the colorful, tempting array of food laid out on the mat. "This is our Polynesian dinner: poi, mangoes, bananas, papaya, pineapple, shrimp, fish, and other fascinating native foods." She nodded toward the grill, which was set under an open window. "The main course is roast suckling pig." A radiant smile lighted her delicate features. "And this is how life will be on your South Seas Island, my love." Still smiling, she said, *"Ia ora na.* That means 'life to you.' It's a greeting."

Nonplussed, Tyler shook his head, as if to clear it. Gail sank to her knees and began spooning poi onto the broad, shiny green leaves set at their places. From the corner of her eye, she watched Tyler. He shed his jacket, loosened his collar, and draped his tie over a palm frond. He undid three buttons on his shirt and sank down onto the floor. Letting out a huge sigh, he reached out a hand toward the food. "I'm starving."

Gently but firmly, Gail grasped his hand and drew it away from the food. "Oh, no, darling. No Polynesian food for outsiders. Only for natives. First you put on your lavalava. *Then* we eat. If we're going to rehearse this scene, we're going to do it right. We must be authentic."

Tyler's expression hardened. Gail stifled a giggle. She knew it wasn't the first time Tyler had discovered that her fragile figure hid a spine of stainless steel. He glared at her, his lips pursed in that stubborn pout she knew so well. Like a little kid, she thought. He must have looked just that way when Daphne told him "No more cookies!" Gail smiled to herself. Somehow she found his expression endearing. She kept her eyes averted, not daring to look at him, in an effort to keep from laughing aloud.

From the corner of her eye, she caught a flash of white as Tyler's shirt fell to the floor, then his T-shirt. She heard the jingle of change in his pockets as his trousers followed. Moments later, clad in the lavalava, looking disgruntled, he dropped down onto the floor across from her, his long legs stretched out before him.

"Tyler!" Gail exclaimed, dismayed. Her gaze was riveted on Tyler's black socks and shining black shoes.

He glanced up at her, eyebrows lifted. "What? What's wrong?"

"Your shoes and socks! You can't wear shoes and socks. It's like putting your feet on our table! And you can't sit that way, either. It's considered rude to stretch out your legs and feet in front of you. You either have to fold them in back of you or sit cross-legged."

A devilish glint came into Tyler's eyes. He stood up, and slowly, with great deliberation, took off his shoes and socks; and with the same slow deliberation he slipped off his red-and-white polka-dot shorts. He placed shoes, socks, and shorts in a neat pile, then sat on the floor across from Gail, his long, hairy legs crossed tailor fashion.

"Tyler!"

Once again his russet brows rose in innocent inquiry. "What's the problem, love?"

Gail blushed furiously. "You're indecent, that's what! You didn't *have* to shed your shorts. Pull down your lavalava!"

Tyler grinned, adjusting his wraparound skirt. "You can't have it both ways, darling. If I can't wear shoes and socks, I can't wear shorts. You don't think the natives wear red-and-white polka-dot shorts, do you?"

"No, but I don't think they go in for indecent exposure, either."

With cheerful nonchalance, Tyler said, "It's all in the eye of the beholder. What's considered indecent exposure here may be perfectly acceptable in Tahiti." He eyed her feathered bosom appreciatively. "Not all the women wear bras, you know. They go around..."

"Tyler," Gail said, speaking with exaggerated patience, "I'm *trying* to help you, to acquaint you with native customs so you won't make a complete fool of yourself, so you'll feel at home..."

Tyler's eyes twinkled with amusement. "Oh? And what makes you an authority on native customs?"

Gail shot him a level, serious look. "I've read all of your brochures, I've scoured the travel books in the library, and I've read all about these places in *National*

Geographic. I know what I'm talking about. Now, you'll probably be invited to a feast or a Sunday *toagai* where chiefs are present, so you need to know what they consider good manners. For instance, you always address a chief from a sitting position."

"Okay, chief. I'm sitting."

Ignoring his jibe, she went on: "And, before eating, wait for grace to be said."

"Grace," Tyler said, bowing his head.

Refusing to let him rattle her, Gail took a deep breath. "You should note the serving of food. As a guest, you will be served first, then the chiefs in order of rank."

"Serve me, woman!"

Gail fixed him with a stern gaze. "Tyler, if you don't practice these things, you may be sorry." She picked up the brown crockery teapot and poured them each a cup of tea. "You never drink a cup of *ava*, which is the traditional beverage, without first tipping a little out of the cup onto the ground in front of you. At the same time you're supposed to say '*manuia*,' which means 'good fortune.'"

Tyler's features set in an expression of mock solemnity. "*Manuia!*" With grave care, he picked up his cup and tipped it forward.

"Tyler!" Gail yelled. "Cut that out!"

He glanced up at her with an injured air. "I'm practicing. You said I should practice."

"Not inside the *house!* You drip it on the *ground!*"

Tyler had the grace to look apologetic. With a corner of his lavalava, he dabbed quickly at the drops of tea that had dripped on the mat. "You should have told me!"

A note of exasperation crept into her voice. "I shouldn't have to tell you everything!"

Tyler reached across the mat. Taking Gail's hand in

his, he gave it a warm squeeze. He smiled deeply into her eyes. "You don't tell me everything. That's what makes you so mysterious, so intriguing, such an endlessly fascinating woman."

Gail flushed. She did have secrets, even from Tyler—that much was true. But it certainly wasn't a deliberate attempt to be mysterious. An only child, she was simply shy. And her lifelong custom of keeping her own counsel had come about because she'd never had anyone with whom to share. At the thought, a wry smile curved her lips. She had come along as a startling surprise, a change-of-life baby to parents who thought children should be seen and not heard.

"Are you going to tell me what all this stuff we're eating is?"

Gail pointed. "This is shrimp."

"I can *see* that! What's this? Looks like potato salad."

"That's marinated raw fish salad. A delicacy."

Gingerly, Tyler put a chunk of the concoction into his mouth and began to chew. At once, his usually calm features contorted in an expression of pain. "Are you trying to poison me?" he exclaimed.

"If I were," Gail said kindly, "you can be sure I'd use something more lethal, and much quicker. Eat up, Tyler. You just have to acquire a taste for some of these foods, and you'd best acquire it before you go." Ignoring the skeptical gleam in his eyes, she went on: "And that's poi, a pudding-baked concoction of arrowroot flavored with banana and a sauce of salted coconut milk. I wanted to make *palusami*—that's a thick coconut cream wrapped in young taro leaves, baked on hot stones and served on slices of baked taro root—but the supermarket was fresh out of young taro leaves."

"Tough!" Tyler remarked.

"And these are yams, and this is hearts-of-palm salad with fresh watercress," Gail said brightly. "Try it, you'll love it. And then you can carve us a little pork."

Tyler gave an emphatic shake of his head. "Not me. I'm not wrestling with any pig! That's woman's work."

"Woman's work!" Gail shrieked. "It may be woman's work in Tahiti, but we're in Connecticut."

Tyler fixed her with an implacable stare. "But we're rehearsing the Tahiti scene, remember?"

Gail's eyes locked with Tyler's. "Okay, okay. I'll carve. But first let's talk about man's work." A mischievous gleam lighted her eyes. "You'll have to do something to keep from being bored, and of course you'll want to earn your keep. From what I've read, you have several choices. For one, you can cut sugarcane in the fields. That way, you'll really get to know the natives, entering into their daily lives..."

"Doesn't appeal to me," Tyler mumbled through a mouthful of poi. "Too physical."

"Or you can climb coconut trees and cut coconuts for copra. Copra's a big crop..."

He gazed at her in mild reproof. "Gail, you know damned well I don't even like to climb a ladder!"

Recalling their tumble from the bittersweet-laden elm, she couldn't argue with that. "How about fishing? Some of the shellfish contain pearls. Or you could cut coral."

"Too dangerous. Coral's sharp. I might cut myself."

"Well, what about deep-sea fishing? You can spend all day in a little boat out on the water in the brilliant sunshine fishing for black marlin, sailfish, ocean bonito, tuna, pompano, red snapper, bass, bonefish..."

"Yes, I might just do that—if I can figure out a way to keep from burning up."

Gail nodded sympathetically. "Poor Tyler. I forgot

you have that tender, fair skin that burns to a crisp." She let out a hopeless sigh. "The only thing left for you to do is to hand-carve wooden figures, or weave straw hats and baskets to sell to passengers on ships that stop at the island."

Tyler snorted. "I'm not into carving and weaving. You're the artistic one in the family."

"Well, then, I guess you'll just have to settle for making *ulasisis*."

Tyler's startled gaze met hers. "Making *what?*"

"*Ulasisis*. They're shell leis." A dreamy look came into her eyes. "I can see you right now, Tyler, combing the beach for shells, then stringing them on a fishline. I'd like a *ulasisi* strung with pink, white, and tan shells. Do you think stringing shells will be too much for you?"

His voice took on a hard edge, giving her warning. "Listen, darling, I can find plenty to do without your help."

Gail lowered her gaze in quick retreat and shifted her line of attack. "Oh, I'm sure you can, Tyler. I mean, you'll have to sweep out the *fale*—that's the thatch-roofed hut the natives live in. Since you're going to live like a child of nature, naturally you'll want to live in a *fale*. They have no walls, of course, but they have open-mat blinds you can lower for protection against violent winds and torrential downpours."

Tyler, munching his hearts of palm, greeted this news with stubborn silence.

"And, of course you'll be busy washing," Gail continued cheerfully. "I read that they do their washing by hand, sitting by an outdoor water spout or a running stream. Cold water, that is, from mountain springs. A hot-water supply is rare. And cooking your meals will take up a lot of your time, because you'll be using an *emu."* She glanced up at Tyler, who was happily popping one shrimp after another into his mouth. Encouraged, she went on.

"The *emu,* an oven, is made of rocks and covered with leaves and burlap sacks. So you'll be building fires, hauling water . . ."

Unperturbed, Tyler said, "Don't concern yourself, darling. I'll hire other people to do all that."

Gail's eyes opened wide in astonishment. "But, Tyler, that would be cheating!"

"Gail!" Tyler roared, startling her out of her wits. "Go carve the pig!"

"Oh, yes, chief," she said, stifling a giggle. "Right away, chief."

Gail carved the pig. When they had finished eating, she put another ukulele tape in the cassette player and sank down across the mat from Tyler. She longed to sit beside him, to snuggle in the cozy curve of his arm, but first came the business at hand.

She let out a long wistful sigh. "This is how life will be on your desert island, Tyler. Peaceful and dreamy and relaxing."

"Right on," Tyler agreed enthusiastically.

Smiling appealingly, she murmured, "And since I've recreated the whole scene, couldn't you just stay here?"

"No, I couldn't, my love."

She felt something shrivel inside her. She swallowed hard, and over a sudden lump in her throat, she persisted. "Well, then, could you settle for an island a bit nearer, like Sherwood Island, or Block Island, or Martha's Vineyard?"

"No, darling. November nineteenth is 'D-Day.'"

A cold hand squeezed her heart. "'D-Day'? Doomsday?" Gail asked numbly.

"Departure Day."

"But, Tyler, I haven't finished your bust! You promised to stay..."

"You promised you'd finish it quickly. Better hurry. You have promises to keep."

And miles to go before I sleep, Gail thought, feeling suddenly desperate. "Oh, I'll hurry, Tyler. Really!" She would make haste...slowly—to keep Tyler here.

AT SCUBA CLASS on the following Tuesday night, everyone took the final diving test, and everyone passed. Gail
emerged from the pool triumphant after swimming her
final twenty-four laps. Happily, she joined her classmates
standing around the side of the pool. They were all laughing and slapping each other on the back and bragging
about how they were going to seek sunken treasure, or
go spearfishing in the Caribbean. Her jubilant mood held
until she heard Tyler remark with an air of casual nonchalance that he'd be diving among the coral reefs in the
South Seas. And when he told everyone he intended to
live there, perhaps indefinitely, he became the star of
the evening. All smiles, he reeled around the pool like
a drunken sailor, tipsy with joy and anticipation. Gail
ground her teeth in silent anguish and said nothing.

Her mood sank to the doldrums when Tyler came
home the next evening and in triumphant tones announced, "Today I gave two weeks' notice. Friday, No-

vember sixteenth, will be my last day at good old Liberty Life!"

"Wonderful," Gail said, forcing a bright, brittle smile. "But I haven't finished your bust." Sudden fire sparkled in her gray eyes. In accusing tones, she went on: "You promised to stay until it was done."

In reproachful tones, he countered, *"You* promised to finish it before I left."

She threw out her hands in a helpless gesture. "I'm sculpting as fast as I can!"

Tyler frowned. "Let's take a look at it."

"It's still pretty rough," she warned. "I have a lot of work to do, polishing your features, your facial expression..."

They trooped upstairs to her airy, glassed-in studio at the back of the house. Tyler stood gazing at his clay head, his face expressionless, rubbing his chin in a thoughtful, judicious way. At last he said, "You've caught the shape of my head all right, and my ears are okay." He turned to face her and locked his arms around her waist, drawing her close against him. Gazing deeply into her eyes, he said gently, "You want the truth, don't you?"

Gail nodded. Her heart thudded furiously.

"The truth is, it isn't the real me."

Her chin quivered and her throat felt dry and tight. "Who is it, Tyler?"

Tyler shrugged. "A stranger. Could be anyone."

Her voice shook. "Tyler, you're very hard to capture—your quick-silver manner, your joie de vivre, your dynamic personality, and at the same time, your calm goodwill, your inner strength and intelligence and nobility. There are so many sides to you, Tyler. It takes time and care to portray all those qualities in one bust."

Tyler nodded sympathetically. "I understand, my love, believe me. Maybe you're trying too hard. Maybe it isn't possible to portray my total personality." He bent his head, kissed the top of her shining hair, and patted her shoulder comfortingly. "Try not to worry, love. After I stop working, I'll *make* more time to sit for you, and I'm sure it will shape up. After all"—he smiled tenderly, smoothing her hair back from her face—"it's only the clay model, not the finished bronze."

Reassured, Gail smiled. But secretly she worried. Was it ever possible for an artist to come up to a man's idea of himself? To make matters worse, Tyler was counting on her to finish. She couldn't let him down. And in her secret heart she knew he would eventually leave, whether the bust was finished or not.

November turned gloomy and gray, matching Gail's somber mood. As each day passed, she grew more distressed. Even the golden leaves had deserted the sugar maple, drifting silently down to earth, leaving black skeletal branches buffeted by the winds.

Early one morning, Gail was seated before Tyler's bust in her sunny studio when a swiftly moving shadow darkened the window. A rush of wings and the sound of lost, lonely cries filled the air. Startled, she dashed to the window. She let out a gasp of mingled pleasure and excitement. The wild geese were flying over, a dark "V" against the gentian sky. They were heading south, sounding their strident, mournful, yet oddly triumphant call. Even the geese are escaping, Gail thought with a slight sense of shock. When the geese flew over, it was a sign that winter was just around the corner. She gave an involuntary shiver. Time was closing in on her! Where in the world was Daphne?

In the days that followed, Gail and Tyler did what they always did at the change of the seasons. Tyler put up the storm windows, put antifreeze in the VW, cleaned out the chimneys, and lugged in more wood, then hung the bird houses and feeders. Gail made seed-and-suet balls for the birds, and housecleaned from attic to cellar, keeping busy, keeping her mind off Tyler's Great Escape. And when she could find nothing else to do, she felt driven to work on Tyler's bust.

She was working on it one sullen gray morning when she was distracted by a sifting of soft white flakes drifting down outside her window. It was unusually early for snow, but she welcomed the first snowfall with the same thrill and excitement she had known as a child.

When she looked outside again at noon, the meadow was hidden under a puffy white quilt. She grinned at a stately bevy of ruffed grouse trailed by a pheasant that strutted indignantly toward the pine woods, and laughed at the antics of chipmunks and squirrels scurrying about under a red oak. A disgruntled-looking skunk and a bright-eyed, nervous raccoon trundled across the meadow, stirred to action by the early snowfall.

Gail flung open the window, reveling in the fresh, cold smell of snow in the air. Eagerly, she held out her hand and caught a few feathery flakes, then stood watching them sparkle, glisten, and melt on her warm palm. Like our marriage, she thought, sparkling, glistening...gone. Shivering with a sudden chill, she closed the window and sat watching the thick snowfall, mesmerized by the swirling flakes. The strident ringing of the phone interrupted her reverie.

Daphne's bright, cheerful voice bubbled across the miles like a sparkling stream. Without preamble, she said, "I've been fishing in Mexico, dear. Just got home.

I do want to see that darling son of mine before he flits off to the wilds."

Daphne's words jarred her so that Gail could scarcely speak. She couldn't believe it! Without a qualm, sensible, down-to-earth Daphne was accepting Tyler's decision to chuck everything and take off. At the same time, feelings of joy and relief coursed through her. "You're coming to Connecticut, then," Gail said eagerly. "Are you leaving Phoenix today?"

"Oh, my dear, I can't leave now."

"But Tyler has only two more days at Liberty Life. He'll be through on the sixteenth, and he'll head for Tahiti as soon as he can get his act together!"

"Can't Tyler delay his departure?" Daphne sounded indignant and demanding at the same time.

"He could," said Gail flatly, "but he won't. You know what he'll say. Time and Tyler wait for no man."

"You tell Tyler P. Peabody he'd better wait for his mother!"

Gail felt she would explode with frustration. "Daphne, please, can't you come *now?*"

"Heavens no, my dear," Daphne said in lilting tones. "I just got home. I'm much too busy catching up. My golf game has suffered horribly. My handicap's as high as a kite. I must get out on the greens. My tennis is terrible. No one will want to play with me if I don't get in a little practice. My bridge is abominable, and my bridge club threatens to drum me out of the corps if I don't show up soon. So you see, Tyler will simply have to wait for me. You tell him both time *and* tide wait for Daphne Peabody, and he'd better wait as well if he ever expects to see *me* again! I'll be there on Thursday, the twenty-second, for Turkey Day, and I'll stay through

Christmas. Bye, bye, dear. God bless." The phone went dead.

Gail dropped the receiver on the hook. Mingled disappointment and confusion surged through her. She sank down in a chair, and at slow speed replayed the conversation with Daphne in her mind. They both knew Daphne could and would jolly well come and go as she pleased. Why had she refused to come now? In an intuitive flash, the truth struck her. Daphne was putting Tyler on the spot, backing him into a corner. Gail burst into laughter. Daphne's bridge might be abominable, her tennis game terrible, her handicap higher than a kite, but she was no slouch in the brains department!

Gail rose from her chair and whirled around the room hugging herself in an explosion of joy. Sidney leaped to his feet and danced at her heels. "Sidney, you salty dog, we've been given a new lease on life! Come on! We're going out to play in the snow!"

They raced around in the swirling snow, tasting the icy flakes on their tongues, rolling side by side down the sloping pasture in back of the red barn. Gail bent down, scooped up a handful of snow, and made a hard-packed snowball. Winding up her right arm, she pitched the missile into the pale sky, shouting, "Go for it, Sid!" Sidney chased gleefully after it, howling with joy. Together they watched the late-fall sun slip behind the blurred hills, spilling golden light on the sparkling, diamond-crusted carpet, while blue and purple finger shadows crept toward the old clapboard house.

Darkness had fallen by the time they stumbled inside, breathless and panting, greeted by the savory aroma of a pot roast Gail had put in the Dutch oven early in the morning. She changed into a fleecy red warm-up suit and hurried to the kitchen. She liked to have dinner ready when Tyler came home. Actually, she enjoyed doing things for Tyler. She liked to please him, to make him happy, simply because she loved him.

In high spirits, Gail turned up the stereo as loud as it would go, belting out Scott Joplin's swinging piano tunes from *The Sting*. Then she set about making Tyler's favorite corn pudding casserole. In a haze of joy and exhilaration, she danced from sink to counter, from stove to table, singing at the top of her lungs: "Da-da-de-da-da-da, da-da-da-da-da-da, de-da-da!" She didn't hear the door open, or see Tyler stride inside.

"Gail!" Tyler thundered.

Gail whirled to face him. He stood in the doorway, ruddy-faced, shoulders powdered with snowflakes, smelling of cold. Happily, she shouted above Scott Joplin, "Oh, darling, I didn't hear you come in."

"I *know!*" Tyler shouted back. "And I know why!" In three quick strides, he crossed the room, turned down the volume on the stereo, then took off his hat and coat and slung them on the hall tree. Clearly, he was as cross as a bear.

Gail ran to greet him. Standing on tiptoes, she flung her arms around his neck and gave him a warm, moist kiss. He responded with an abstracted peck. His expression called to her mind one of the great stone faces carved on Mount Rushmore.

"It's snowing," he grumbled. "Big, thick, dry flakes. Cars are sliding all over the road. Not many people have snow tires on in November." Indignation sharpened his tone. "It has no right to snow this early in the year." He stamped his feet emphatically on the string rug by the door. "Thank God it doesn't snow in Tahiti. But it might!" he added irritably. "You can't count on *anything* these days!" He went to stand before the fire, rubbing his hands together and staring moodily at the yellow flames crackling on the hearth.

Swiftly, Gail carried the corn pudding from oven to table. "Darling, the most wonderful thing happened today. Someone reached out and touched us!"

"Not the phone company again!"

"Daphne!" Gail spoke his mother's name as if she were giving Tyler a gift. "She's coming to visit! And staying till after Christmas."

Tyler brightened. "Wonderful! But she's always come for Christmas. I'm glad she's carrying on the tradition."

"This year she's going all out. She's hell-bent on seeing you before you leave. She'll be here the twenty-second."

"Gail," Tyler said in ominous tones, "I won't be here on December twenty-second."

"Oh, but she'll be here on *November* twenty-second." Gail's voice brimmed with cheerful goodwill.

Tyler spun to face her. A troubled frown furrowed his brow.

"Daphne will be terribly disappointed if you're not here. She said..." Gail paused, hating to deliver Daphne's threat verbatim. "She said you may never see her again."

With an air of defeat, Tyler slumped down onto a chair. "I know. I know." He let out a long, resigned sigh. "I mean, she's getting on in years. After all, sixty-one is no spring chicken. I can't simply walk out on the old dear. I'll just have to postpone my trip a few days."

Gail felt like cheering. Instead, she silently blessed Daphne, thinking: It's a wise mother who knows her own child.

Grumpily, Tyler went on: "You can't count on *anything* these days!"

Gail went to him and put an arm around his shoulders. "Oh, you're so right, Tyler. But try not to fret. As someone—I don't know who—said, 'All things happen for the best, and every cloud has a silver lining.'"

Tyler gave her a friendly swat on the bottom. "I'll be watching for that silver lining, darling, day and night."

During dinner, Tyler lapsed into a moody silence, interrupted only by Gail's valiant efforts to make conversation. She told Tyler about the birds she'd seen, the red flash of the cardinal and the chickadees, juncos, and blue jays crowding around the feeders. And the skunks and raccoons she and Sid had watched trundling across the meadow, Sid whining to chase them. "I saw squirrels, too. They were putting nuts away for the winter," she said brightly.

"Hmm," Tyler said.

She tried a new tack. "This morning I reshaped your nose." She tried to sound enthusiastic. "I think I've at last achieved that rare combination of strength of purpose, nobility, and dignity that is the real you!"

Tyler refused to be cheered up. Gail understood. Tyler was a man who, having made a decision, acted upon it. He did not take kindly to his plans being foiled.

His dour mood persisted throughout dinner. Afterward, he plunked down in his rocker. Scowling, he took up his pen to work the crossword puzzle. That he hadn't retreated to his study to work clearly showed how distraught he was. Further evidence of his grouchy state was that he didn't even ask Gail the word for African antelope, which he could never remember. Gail attacked the pink tulip in her quilting frame. A tense silence invaded the room. The ticking of the mantel clock sounded as loud as a ticking time bomb.

At length, Gail could stand the tension no longer. She

flung down her needlework, jumped up from her chair, and peered out the window. In firm, decisive tones, she said, "I'm going out for a little while, Tyler."

"Out!" Tyler exclaimed, as if not knowing the meaning of the word.

"Out," Gail said flatly.

"Out, where?" Tyler demanded.

"Outside."

At that Sidney leaped up from the braided wool rug and danced about, ready to go.

"It's *snowing* outside!"

"It's stopped snowing," Gail said calmly. "I'm going for a ride."

He looked up from his puzzle, his eyes filled with concern. "I don't think you should take the car out, Gail. The roads are terribly slippery. It's too dangerous."

"I'm not taking the car. I'm taking Sidney. We're going for a ride in his sled."

Tyler did a double take, staring at her in disbelief. "Not that old dogsled we bought last year at the auction!"

Gail grinned. "You've got it, Tyler. Dogsled. A light, low, wood-framed vehicle, two feet wide and six feet long with steel runners."

"You need a *team* of dogs. Sidney can't pull that thing!"

"Of course he can. I trained him to pull it last winter to amuse myself while you were on the road. Lee and Mel Fishback's *Novice Sled Dog Training* told us all we needed to know."

Astonishment lighted his eyes. "Why didn't you tell me?"

A swift blush stained her cheeks. "I'd planned to surprise you. But by the time Sidney and I really learned to mush, there wasn't a decent snow. Anyway, when the snow was too deep to drive the car, Sid and I drove the sled to the village, and he hauled food home from the supermarket. He knows 'sit,' 'stay,' 'mush,' and 'whoa!' He's not too swift with 'gee' and 'haw,' but he'll learn. Pulling a sled is his mission in life, an inborn trait handed down from his ancestors."

Tyler appeared dumbfounded. Before he could speak, she went on: "Sidney's a born lead dog—intelligent, strong, and hardy. He's big, broad in the chest, and has a good bushy tail for balance." She fixed her gaze on Sidney. "Come on, Sid. Let's hit the trail." Without another word to Tyler, she marched from the room.

Minutes later, Gail, wearing a sky-blue, fur-trimmed parka, beige wool slacks over her warm-up suit, and black mukluks on her feet, returned to the keeping room. To her astonishment, Tyler stood leaning against the doorframe, his arms crossed over his chest. He was garbed for the outdoors in his red woolen cap, the earflaps pulled snugly down over his ears, and a fleece-lined Loden jacket and boots.

"I can't let you go out in the dark and the snow alone, darling," he explained. "And I want to see Sidney in action."

Gail grinned. "Don't worry, Sid knows the old pasture cow path like the back of his paw."

They stepped outside into a splash of brilliant starlight that brightened the entire countryside, then trudged down to the barn. When they brought the harness and sled out onto the gravel turnaround, Sidney perked up his ears and yelped excitedly.

"See that, Tyler! He remembers! He loves being lead dog, even without a team. Gives him a sense of purpose in life." In the pale cone of light over the barn door, Gail straddled Sidney, slipped on his harness, and snapped it to the outer edges of the long, low sled. He strained forward, eyes bright with anticipation, raring to go. "Sidney, sit!" Gail commanded. Sidney sat.

Gail moved quickly to the back of the sled, pressed the brake down, and let it snap. She gave the sled a little push forward to get it going, and at the same time shouted, "Mush, Sidney, mush!"

Head and tail low, back humped, Sidney bolted forward and headed down the cow path toward the snowy meadow. Gail gripped the handlebars and hung on like glue, riding the back runners. Sidney quickly settled into a steady trot. From the corner of her eye, Gail saw Tyler running beside her with a long, loping stride, grinning from ear to ear.

"Good show!" he shouted, his face wreathed in smiles. Gail felt a flood of happiness surge through her.

They moved at a swift, steady pace, Sidney's wide, furry feet skimming lightly over the snow-crusted ground. The thin pale moon drenched the meadow with pure silvery light. The distant wooded hills looked ghostly, studded with wraithlike trees trimmed in white ermine.

Gail clung to the handlebars and shifted her weight from side to side, steering the sled. She breathed deeply of the biting-cold air that stung her cheeks, and drew the hood of her parka more closely about her face. She reveled in the silence that seemed to echo around them, like the hollow sound she heard when she pressed an ear to a conch shell.

Keeping her eye on the trail, she saw a rocky patch of ground ahead. Quickly, she pressed her foot lightly on the brake and shifted her weight. "Haw, Sidney, haw!" Sidney veered left around it, then back on the cow path. "Good boy!" Gail shouted. Pridefully, she glanced at Tyler, yelling, "He did it! He knows left and right!"

Tyler raised a circled thumb and forefinger in a gesture of admiration.

Sidney crested a small rise with ease, then broke into a run down the long, sloping hill. The wind whipped their faces, stung their eyes. Breathless, exhilarated, Gail shouted, "This is the life! Right, Tyler?"

"Terrific!" Tyler shouted.

Gail noticed that he was huffing and puffing, and had fallen slightly behind. Laughing, she closed her eyes and lifted her face to the cold, crisp air. Suddenly, she felt the sled gain momentum. Her eyes flew open. Faster and faster, the sled careened down the hillside. For a fraction of a second, she froze. The sled was gaining on Sidney. His bushy tail curled up over his back, waving like a signal flag.

Swiftly, Gail pressed her foot on the brake, but Sidney raced on with long, powerful strides, streaking downhill. Gail clung to the handlebars of the flying sled like a drowning victim clutching a life preserver. She heard a blood-chilling scraping sound. At the same instant, the sled rocked violently from side to side, then gave a sickening lurch.

"Watch out!" Tyler yelled, too late.

Gail felt herself hurtling through space. She landed with a thud on her bottom in the thick snow. She heard Tyler shouting frantically, "Stop, Sidney, stop!" Sidney dashed on, dragging the overturned sled behind him.

"Whoa! Sid, whoa!" Gail shouted.

In the clear white starlight, she saw Sidney come to a halt and look over his shoulder at the overturned sled, as if to say, What's the matter with you two, anyway?

"Good boy!" Gail yelled. "Good boy!"

Tyler hunkered down beside her and swept her up in his arms. "Gail, love, are you all right?"

Gail burst into laughter. "Right as rain—or snow. But Sidney looks so surprised, and so disgusted. He can't figure out what happened. Sit, Sid. Stay."

Sidney threw her a reproachful look and sank down on his stomach, resting his head on his paws.

"He was going great till you hit that stone slab," Tyler said worriedly. "Your hood's fallen off." He reached up and smoothed Gail's hair, touching her head tenderly. "How about you? Any bumps or gashes?"

Gail thumped her head. "Sound as a pumpkin."

"You scared the wits out of me. I was afraid you'd conked your noggin on the rock and were down for the count."

Gail laughed. "Tyler, you know how hard-headed I am."

His gaze met hers, sparkling with amusement. "You can say that again!"

Tyler brushed the snow from her hood and shoulders. His lips curved in a broad smile. "You look like an Eskimo."

"Eskimos rub noses," Gail said, nuzzling Tyler's nose.

"Your nose is cold."

Gail chuckled. "That means I'm healthy." Her lips grazed his cheek.

"Mmm, your lips are cold. What's that mean?"

"Means I have a warm heart."

His mouth came down on hers, warm and loving. "I think the saying is, 'Cold hands, warm heart.'"

"My hands are cold, too." She stripped off her gloves and placed a hand on each of his cheeks. "Feel."

"Ow!" Tyler howled. "They're freezing!" He unzipped his jacket and, clasping her hands in his, pressed them against his warm chest.

"Much better," Gail murmured. Snuggling closer, she

burrowed inside his jacket, burying her face against his shoulder.

He wrapped his jacket around them, enclosing them both in its fleece-lined warmth. Softly, he said, "I can feel your heart going pit-a-pat."

Gail laughed. "Not through my parka. It must be *your* heart going pit-a-pat."

"Well, let's see." His good-natured, bantering tone turned low and tender, husky with emotion. He slid a hand inside his jacket and, parting Gail's parka, pushed up the top of her warm-up suit. He bent his head, as if the better to see in the thin, silvery moonlight. She could feel his warm breath on her cheek, smell the fresh, cold snowdrops sparkling in his russet hair. Dreamily, she became aware of a few lazy snowflakes drifting down. One or two came to rest on her midriff, glistening on her bare skin. At once Tyler kissed them away. With loving hands, he caressed her face, her throat, her breasts.

A rush of love for Tyler flowed through her, and with it, mounting desire. She moved sensuously under his touch. His strong, gentle fingers traveled downward, around her waist, roamed up her spine, stroking her back. "Your skin is so soft and smooth, so lustrous, it glows with the fine patina of..."

A spark of devilment glistened in her eyes. "Tyler, you were listening to my heart, and my heart still lives on my left side, front."

At once his hand returned to the region of her heart. She breathed an ecstatic sigh. Unbuttoning Tyler's shirt, she ran her hands over the soft, springy hair covering his chest.

"Tyler," she murmured, her lips brushing his ear, "you're right. Your heart isn't going pit-a-pat. It's going thump, thump, thump, pounding down the fast track."

"A runaway horse," Tyler murmured, imprisoning her lips with his own. His tongue, seeking, exploring, her warm, moist mouth, found an eager response. Her ardor rose to match his. She clung to him as he stretched out on the snowy hillside, snug and warm in their sheepskin cocoon. His sensitive hands slid over her breasts, moving downward. As if fingering a flute, Tyler tickled her ribs.

Laughter bubbled on her lips. "Tyler! You'd better quit runaway-horsing around, or you're going to be in big trouble."

She gave him a playful poke.

"Whatever you say, darling." His nimble fingers fastened on the waistband of her warm-up suit, sliding it down around her hips.

"Tyler!" Gail shrieked. "What do you think you're doing?"

His laughter rang out, echoing across the starlit meadow. "I've quit horsing around. This is serious!" He curved his big, warm hands about her hips and bent his head, strewing light, feathery kisses across her abdomen.

Gail clapped her hands over his ears, pulling his head up level with hers. "Kiss me, sweet thing."

"Whatever you say, love."

His mouth claimed hers, responding to her eager kisses. She felt his hands caressing her skin, warming each curve and crevice of her body, arousing her hunger for him so that every nerve ending tingled with desire. Just when she thought she couldn't endure the ecstasy of his caresses another second, he ended her torment, taking her in a blazing burst of passion that left her breathless, reeling with delight, reveling in the sweet bliss of consummating their love.

She had no idea how long she lay enfolded in Tyler's arms in the shelter of his sheepskin coat, steeped in a drowsy dreaming state, when she heard Sidney whimper, felt his cold nose nuzzling her ear. She sat up and patted Sidney's head.

"It's okay, Sidney. We're not freezing to death on the tundra. We're lovers. Lovers do crazy things." She poked Tyler in the ribs. "Come on, Tyler. Sidney's worried about us. And I think he wants to go home."

They righted the sled and Gail and Sidney took off at a sedate trot, with Tyler jogging beside them. Gail felt light-headed, giddy with joy and happiness. Making love with Tyler was one of the best things about their marriage. And when Tyler was gone, she thought dolefully, she would miss their lovemaking like—as much as J. Alfred Prufrock would miss water. Just thinking about it made her heart swell with pain. She wrestled with the problem all the way back to the barn.

After Gail and Tyler had stashed away the harness and sled and were walking hand in hand back to the house, she said sadly, "Tyler, it's going to be terribly hard to make it through the long, lonely days and nights without ever being as one."

Tyler gave her hand a comforting squeeze. "I know, my love. I feel the same way, too. But I'll manage, and so will you. I have the utmost trust in you. It isn't in you to be unfaithful."

"That's true, Tyler," Gail agreed regretfully. "So we're just going to have to learn to deny ourselves."

Tyler halted midstride, staring down at her. For a long moment, he was speechless. When at last he spoke, his voice cracked in incredulous disbelief. "We're going to have to do *what?*"

"Learn to deny ourselves," Gail said firmly. "We must get used to doing without before you go, so it won't be such a hardship after you've gone."

Tyler's jaw set in obstinate refusal. "That's the craziest idea I've ever heard!"

She started to say that it wasn't the craziest idea *she* had ever heard. Instead, in tones that brooked no argument, she said quietly, "I, too, have to get ready for your leaving, and that's the way of it."

Tyler made no reply. She couldn't read his reaction: whether he'd accepted her decision, or whether he thought, we'll just see about that! He would see soon enough that she meant what she said. She *had* noticed a luminous light sparkling in Tyler's sherry-colored eyes during their romantic interlude. Maybe, just maybe, he'd decide to stay home. It was a feeble hope. She couldn't count on it. Not this time. She would see what tomorrow would bring.

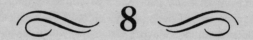

8

GAIL WAS NOT happy with what tomorrow brought, for it brought Tyler down, flat on his back in their four-poster bed with a terrible cold that made his eyes water and his nose run. Violent sneezes shook Tyler's back teeth and set her own on edge.

Ignoring his protests that he felt fine, Gail doctored him. She kept a fire blazing in the hearth in their bedroom. She set hot bricks wrapped in a towel in the bed to warm his feet. In the morning, she made beef broth, which had been her mother's sure cure for colds, then stood at his side watching to make sure he drank it. Throughout the morning, she offered him hot tea, cola, and pineapple, grapefruit, apple, and orange juices. In reply, he made frightful faces, which she took to be a refusal.

At noon, having suddenly recalled that one was supposed to "starve a cold and feed a fever," she gave Tyler no lunch. As the afternoon wore on and he seemed no better, she concluded she'd made a mistake. It must be, "feed a cold and starve a fever." Desperate, she decided to try Dear Abby's old standby, chicken soup. Starting from scratch, she made a kettleful of chicken soup for Tyler. At suppertime, she carried a bowl of the hot, savory-smelling soup to his bedside. "Wolf this down, Tyler, and you'll be baying at the moon."

Grumbling, Tyler forced down a few sips. But by nine o'clock that night, he seemed no better. Gail, a total stranger to illness, decided drastic measures must be taken.

From her shelf of recipe books in the hutch, she took down a notebook of Tyler's favorite recipes that Daphne had copied in her own hand. Frantically, Gail flipped through the pages, hoping the one she needed would be there. She let out an exultant whoop. On the last page, she found Daphne's Never-Fail Head-Cold Prescription. Ten minutes later, she carried upstairs to Tyler a steaming, fragrant hot toddy, heavily laced with whiskey.

In sympathetic tones, Gail said, "Since you missed out on these all day, I made it a double."

Grinning, Tyler raised himself up on his elbows, sniffing appreciatively. He took the cup in his hand and lifted it in salute. "Here's to you, kid," he croaked.

While he sipped the hot brew, Gail collected an armload of patchwork quilts from the dower chest and began spreading them over Tyler's lean body.

"Hey, what do you think you're doing? I'm already roasting like a pig in a pit!"

Relentlessly, Gail threw on another quilt. "You've got it, darling. This is the second part of your mother's Never-Fail Prescription. We're going to roast that cold right out of your head."

"Enough is enough!" Tyler shouted testily. He grabbed

the top quilt and tossed it on the floor.

Gail gave him a calm, steely smile. "You are in no condition to make important decisions. I'll decide when enough is enough." She bent down, picked up the quilt, and flung it over Tyler, tucking it in snugly around him.

"You're smothering me!" he shouted.

Gail continued to smile. "Sometimes the cure is worse than the ailment, love. Besides, suffering makes us strong. Who said that, anyway?"

Tyler groaned and lay back down on the pillow. "I don't know, and I don't care!"

Miraculously, before Gail's watchful eyes, Tyler's health seemed to improve. By bedtime, when she crawled in beside him, he seemed quite jovial.

Cheerfully, he gathered up the quilts and tossed them on the floor, then curved an arm around Gail's shoulders, drawing her close to his side. Nuzzling her ear, he murmured huskily, "I don't need all those quilts with you here beside me. 'I've got my love to keep me warm.' Frank Sinatra."

Snuggling closer, Gail said softly, "Oh, Tyler, I'm really going to miss you when you're gone. I'll feel like a fish out of water. Without you, this old four-poster will be much too wide and too cold."

In sympathetic tones, Tyler said, "I understand, love. It's going to be hard for you at first, but you'll get used to it in time."

"Of course I will!" Gail agreed a bit too heartily. "As you say, we owe it to ourselves to be all we can be." Her voice rose on a cheerful note of optimism. "And of course I'll be much happier in the long run."

Tyler responded with heavy silence.

Into Gail's mind, like sheep jumping a fence, leaped all the things she may have done to alienate Tyler, to drive him from home. Maybe she shouldn't have painted their front door Christmas-red for the holidays last year, as a happy surprise greeting for Tyler when he came home. He had been surprised, but not happy. Guiltily, she recalled that he'd had to slap on three coats of Colonial white to cover it.

Or maybe she shouldn't have bought the Queen Anne highboy she'd fallen in love with—even though it had been a steal—which had taken Tyler two years to refinish. After all, the attic was crammed with antiques they'd inherited from three generations of both their families. But he had seemed to enjoy refinishing the highboy and his Lincoln rocker, as well. Actually, he seemed happiest in his holey T-shirt, threadbare jeans, and sneakers, taking off an hour now and then, scraping and sanding and steel-wooling in the barn.

Maybe she shouldn't have called Daphne to arms. With the suddenness of a lightning bolt, an appalling thought struck her. Tyler was the apple of Daphne's eye. Tyler could do no wrong. Would Daphne side with Tyler, or with Gail in her battle to keep him home? Yes, she decided ruefully, calling on Daphne had been a risky move. A shiver shook her from head to toe. She might well fall into the pit she had dug for Tyler! At once she reassured herself. If nothing else, Daphne's visit would gain her more time to bring Tyler to his senses. At last she drifted off to sleep, comforted by Tyler's wheezing snores.

Even the weather conspired to remind Gail that time was running out. The trees all shed their leaves, except for the oaks, whose rich, wine-red finery clung tenaciously, and turned spice brown. There came a severe, killing frost, and the musty smell of fallen leaves gave way under gray metallic skies, and rain fell in long, leaden lines. It was only by a supreme effort of will that Gail managed to keep up her spirits, for in her heart she knew that Daphne was her last line of defense. In anticipation of her mother-in-law's visit, Gail made a fragrant potpourri of dried rose petals and spices to fill the ginger jar in the parlor, and hung a welcoming bunch of yellow, rust, and purple Indian corn woven with spears of golden wheat on the front door.

By noon on Thanksgiving Day, the turkey was dressed, the yams cooked, the butternut squash casserole and the mince pie made. All was in readiness for Daphne's arrival. Early in the afternoon Gail donned her best creamy silk blouse, rust plaid woolen skirt, hose, and heels. Tyler gave up his holey sweat shirt for a hunter-green sport shirt and tan cords. At four o'clock, when dusk was falling, they settled down in the keeping room and, buoyed by an air of cheerful excitement and anticipation, kept an ear cocked for the sound of Daphne's Mercedes convertible roaring up the lane.

Tyler tossed fat pine kindling on the open fire and sank down in his Lincoln rocker. It came to Gail that sitting here with Tyler, toasting before the fire, gave her a sense of peace and pleasure, as if all were right with her world. She gazed lovingly at Tyler, sitting with his head back, eyes closed. Was he dreaming of his South Seas island? A swift stab of pain clouded her eyes. Her chin rose. She wanted to shout at him, "Here, here, none of that while I'm around!" And her soul cried out, "Don't leave me now, in your mind and heart, my love, before it's even time for you to go!"

She jumped to her feet, put *Elvira Madigan* on the cassette deck, then crossed to Tyler. Standing before him, she leaned down and, placing her fingertips on his temples, rubbed his head in a soothing, circular motion. His eyes remained closed. Gail chuckled. He wasn't above pretending to be asleep if he thought she'd keep on massaging his head.

"Tyler, are you playing possum?" He sat as still as a millpond. She reached out a hand and grasped the back of the rocker, swaying it gently, to and fro.

Suddenly, a jubilant shout exploded in the peaceful stillness of the keeping room. "Gotcha!" At the same time, two powerful arms closed about Gail, and Tyler pulled her down into his lap.

She let out a startled shriek. "Unhand me, villain!"

Tyler burst out laughing. "That's called the pincers movement!"

Gail's eyes twinkled with laughter. She rested her head on his shoulder and snuggled closer against him. "It certainly immobilizes the victim."

"Exactly my intention," Tyler agreed, clearly pleased with himself.

"Hmm. Exactly what *are* your intentions?"

Tyler smiled broadly and a wicked glint came into his eyes. "Strictly dishonorable. Honorable intentions are no fun at all." He slid an arm under her knees and draped her legs over the arm of the rocker. He took up his pen and, holding each of her hands in turn, with great care made a tiny "X" on each palm. "There," he said, as if satisfied with a job well done, "I've put my mark on you forever."

"That's lovely, Tyler." Gail put a hand on either side of his face and kissed him full on the lips. "You sweet thing." But when she would have drawn back, she felt the gentle pressure of his hand on the back of her head, holding her captive in his tender embrace. His kiss deepened, and a warm, sweet sensation, like melted chocolate, flowed all through her. The spicy fragrance of his Lagerfeld after-shave lotion mingled with the seductive fragrance of her *Toujours Moi* perfume. *Toujours Moi!* How ironic, she thought with a wry smile, that Tyler should have given me a perfume that translates as "Always Me."

Tyler's free hand slid in a slow, sensuous path down the smooth silken length of her legs, brushing the tender skin around her ankles, then traveled slowly upward, circling her knees, trailing along her thigh, exploring the enticing curves of softly rounded hip and slender waist. She wound her arms about his neck and reached up, running her fingers through his hair, stroking the back of his neck, kneading the taut muscles. She leaned into him and heard his swift intake of breath as her breasts pressed against his chest. A warning spark ignited inside her like a signal fire. She mustn't let things get out of hand. She drew back, holding her body stiffly away from him.

The next instant, Tyler's loving fingers freed the buttons at the V neck of her creamy silk blouse. His hands curved about her high, firm breasts. His thumbs, moving in sensuous circles, teased the tips to life.

With one quick motion, Gail grabbed Tyler's wrists, crossed them on her lap, and held them in a tight grip. Slowly, relentlessly, she shook her head.

"Tyler, have you forgotten already?"

He looked baffled, and a little hurt. "Forgotten? I haven't forgotten Mother's coming, if that's what you mean. But she's not just going to walk in on us, straight through our solid oak front door! She's going to knock first, and then she's going to wait for me to open it, because it's locked. So relax." He bent his head, and his mouth, warm, seeking, covered hers. He wrenched his wrists from her grasp. His arms closed protectively around her. His fingers loosened the hooks on her bra.

Gail drew a deep breath to steady her resolve. Tyler left no doubt that he wanted her with all his heart and soul. And she wanted him. Oh, how she wanted him! Her entire being ached with wanting him, wanting to be lost in each other, wanting to make the world go away so there were only the two of them, spinning, whirling, in space, wrapped in their all-consuming love. She drew another breath. With a valiant effort of will, she clutched Tyler's arms, tugging them away, twisting from his rapturous embrace.

Tyler jerked bolt upright, his good-natured features contorted in a baffled, wounded expression. "Hey, what gives? Don't you believe the door's locked, that Daphne won't burst in on us?"

"I believe you, Tyler." A mischievous gleam lighted her eyes. "When we're making love, I wouldn't care if the Music Man and seventy-six trombones walked in on us!"

Tyler's mouth quirked in a lopsided grin. "You can say that again!"

"When we're making love I wouldn't care if—"

"I know, I know." His smile faded. A puzzled frown furrowed his brow; an injured expression clouded his eyes. "So what's wrong?"

"Nothing's wrong," she said gently. "Nothing at all. You've just forgotten that we must learn to deny ourselves."

An amused, skeptical glint appeared in his eyes. "Speak for yourself, woman."

"I *am* speaking for myself. But *you* are going away. And since you're going away, I must learn to deny my passions." Her soft lips curved in a wistful smile. "I'm only trying to help you to do the same."

As if thrown off balance, unable to decide whether to laugh or growl, Tyler swept a distracted hand through his russet hair. All at once, like a wounded bear, he bellowed, "That's crazy—and totally unnecessary! You're hurting both of us, and for no reason. I don't understand why you're doing this!"

Gail looked him directly in the eyes. In quiet, implacable tones, she said, "Because I feel it's necessary. Desperation is the mother of necessity."

Tyler lifted his hands and let them drop on the arms of the rocker in a helpless gesture. "Gail, if I didn't feel like howling, I'd laugh. What you mean to say is, 'Necessity is the mother of invention.'"

"That, too," Gail replied cheerfully. Once again she captured Tyler's wrists in a tight, two-handed grip, and then leaned back, relaxing against his forest-green wool-clad chest. She nestled her cheek in the comfortable curve between his shoulder and jaw and stared dreamily into the bright crimson, orange, and old-gold flames crackling on the hearth.

Tyler rested his cheek on the top of her glossy black hair. After a deep, thoughtful silence, he mumbled, "Sometimes you can give a person more help than he really wants."

Gail suppressed the quick laughter bubbling inside her. "That's true, Tyler," she said soberly. "Very true!"

Tyler drew a breath that seemed to start at the bottom of his toes, erupting in a long, frustrated sigh. He nuzzled Gail's cheek and, saying no more, stared moodily into the leaping flames.

The shelf clock was striking a quarter past four when they heard Daphne's convertible roar up the lane. They jumped up from the rocker and ran to the front door.

Privately, Gail agreed with Tyler that Daphne was not the sort of woman who simply walked inside a house. Opening the door to Daphne was like opening a bottle of champagne. She burst through the doorway sparkling with blond, radiant beauty, bubbling with joy. She flung her arms about Gail, in a mighty hug, then hugged Tyler, laughing and exclaiming happily, "Oh, it's so *good* to see you! So *good* to be here!"

Smiling, Gail clasped Daphne's shoulders and held her at arm's length. "You look pretty good yourself!" Her fond gaze swept Daphne's short, slender figure from her head, where not one thread of silver was permitted among the short wavy golden-blond tresses, down her fashionable toasty-beige tweed suit and apricot cashmere sweater, to her stylishly shod feet. Her erect carriage, her trim, firm figure and fine, golden-tanned skin that accentuated the vivid blue of her eyes all belied her sixty-one years.

When the greetings were over and Tyler had brought in Daphne's luggage, they strolled into the parlor to warm themselves before the hickory fire blazing in the hearth. Daphne admired Gail's bittersweet arrangement in the Chinese brass bowl, sniffed the potpourri appreciatively, then sank down in the rose brocade wing chair like visiting royalty presiding over the room. Rather like the Queen of Hearts visiting Alice in Wonderland, Gail thought, stifling a grin. Recalling Daphne's passion for drinking tea from breakfast to bedtime, Gail started toward the kitchen.

"I'm going to make you a pot of tea, Daphne. I found a new variety, Keemun Congu—you'll love it. It'll warm the cockles of your heart."

Daphne's brows rose. She pushed back the cuff of her tweed jacket and glanced at her watch.

"It's four-thirty," Tyler said, "on the nose."

"Hmm," said Daphne. "As a matter of fact, I allow myself a little nip of Chivas Regal, now and again." Her lips curved in an impish grin. "That would *really* warm the cockles of my heart."

"Daphne," Tyler said evenly, "the sun's not over the yardarm. We don't have cocktails till five."

Daphne cocked her head, regarding him judiciously. "My, you *are* locked into the clock, aren't you!" With a saucy lift of her chin, she sang out gaily, "But it's five o'clock somewhere!"

Oh, Lord, thought Gail. She's playing right into his hands, with her locked-into-the-clock talk! She cast a nervous glance at Tyler. If he was surprised by his strait-laced mama's thirst for Chivas Regal, he was hiding it well. But after he returned to the parlor with their drinks and they had sipped a bit and everyone began to relax, it occurred to Gail that he might have preferred, might even have been relieved, to see his outspoken mother feeling a little tiddly, a bit mellow. All the better to pull the wool over her eyes and get her on his team, thought Gail savagely.

Gail and Tyler listened spellbound while Daphne told them about her adventures in Mexico: how she'd fished for grouper, climbed ancient pyramids, and explored crumbling ruins in the dark, mysterious jungles of the Yucatán. When she finished, Tyler, carefully avoiding Gail's gaze, stared directly at Daphne. In studied, casual tones, he said, "I have an announcement."

Gail suddenly felt cold all over. She stiffened, holding her breath. Would Daphne go along with Tyler? Would she give him her good wishes, her blessing, in his hare-brained plan, or would she try to talk some sense into his head?

In ringing, decisive tones, filled with a sense of purpose, Tyler said, "I've resigned from my job and I'm going to live on a desert island."

Daphne burst into peals of exuberant laughter that seemed to touch the open-beamed ceiling and bounce back again, echoing through the room. Gasping for breath, she clapped a hand to her bosom. After several moments, she managed to regain her voice. Aping Tyler's ringing, decisive tones, she said, "Tyler, that's the silliest idea I've ever heard!"

Gail, slightly tiddly herself, feeling like the Cheshire cat viewing the scene from the safety of a limb high in a tree, grinned from ear to ear. Surely, Tyler would listen to reason from his strong-minded mother!

Tyler set his glass down hard on the Pembroke end table and set his jaw in that obstinate way Gail knew so well. A crimson flush crept up his neck over his face, into his hairline. Plainly incensed by his mother's frivolous attitude, by her refusal to take him seriously, he looked her squarely in the eye. Sternly, he said, "This is a thing I must do."

Again Daphne burst into peals of laughter, tossing a beringed hand in an airy wave of dismissal. "What utter nonsense!"

Tyler jumped to his feet to stand before her. His lean, sinewy figure towered over his petite mother, who presided from the rose brocade wing chair. In tones that were kind, and at the same time as firm, as unyielding, as immovable as Plymouth Rock, he said, "My decision is made. With or without your approval, I'm going to fulfill my destiny."

His solemn, lofty air reminded Gail of a British barrister handing down a decision. "Hear! Hear!" she cried, clapping her hands.

Daphne cocked her head, fixing her son with a flinty blue gaze. In frigid tones, she said, "Tyler, I did not deed you this house, handed down through generations of the Peabody family, only for you to abandon it. I'm afraid, my boy, that I will have to take it back, snatch the roof from over your head, cut the ground from under your feet, so to speak."

Tyler leaned toward her, the light of freedom blazing in his eyes. "That's A-okay with me! You've hit the trouble right on the head. My life is ruled by *things*. Things are an intolerable burden. Gail, you, me—we're all imprisoned, enslaved by *things*."

Gail saw Daphne stiffen and start to bristle. But she felt only relief that the older woman was at last beginning to see that it wouldn't be easy to change Tyler's mind. Talking him out of his Great Escape was going to be a challenge, a battle of wits to the end.

Daphne fixed her son with a stern, uncompromising stare.

"Listen, Tyler, most of us feel caged in some way, all our lives. Walls, bars, and fences are there whether we can see them or not. We all long for a fling at freedom outside the restrictions of our existence. It seems we're always climbing over obstacles. But that's what life is all about, climbing over obstacles."

Tyler shook his head. "I've done that, dear heart."

Daphne's tone grew hard and sharp with vexation. "People do not simply walk out on their lives!"

Tyler's mouth curved in a maddening, self-assured grin. "That's only because they haven't the courage. *I* do!"

Daphne drew herself up to her most majestic height. "Listen, Tyler, you're forgetting who you are!" Her voice rose to a commanding shout. "You are a Peabody!"

"A *some*body!" Gail put in enthusiastically.

Disconcerted, Daphne shot Gail a reproving glance, and continued her tirade. "A Connecticut Peabody! You must consider your heritage, Tyler! Remember, it is your privilege and your duty to uphold the family name. Your dear father and I reared you to be a responsible person, dependable, forthright, high-principled, an upstanding citizen. We sent you to the best schools and the Episcopalian Church..."

"And brought me up on the Bible and Shakespeare," interrupted Tyler, beaming benevolently at Daphne. "To thine own self be true, Mother, dear. I'm going to look for the real me. I'm going to *be* the real me, instead of being what people have told me I am. I'm going to be true to myself."

"What about being true to Gail?" Daphne snapped.

"I am true to Gail," Tyler said staunchly.

Daphne's head spun to face Gail. "Don't tell me you're going along with Tyler's folly!"

Dispiritedly, Gail replied, "Tyler doesn't want me to go along with his folly. He wants to go alone."

Daphne's eyes flashed blue fire. Her voice rose in outraged indignation. "And when are you filing for divorce?"

"Divorce!" Gail and Tyler exclaimed together in appalled tones.

"I have no intention of divorcing Gail," Tyler said self-righteously. "She is the perfect wife..."

"I'm not asking *you*, you backslider. I'm asking Gail."

"Gail is not asking for a divorce, Mother. You don't understand..."

"Indeed I don't, you sluggard! Whom do you expect to take care of things while you're off lolling on the beach at Bora Bora?"

"I was thinking more of Pago Pago or Papeete."

"Wherever! Who will take over your responsibilities? Who will shovel the snow? Who will fix the furnace? Who will lug in the wood?"

Tyler aimed a confident smile at Gail. "Gail is perfectly capable of taking care of everything. She has the courage, the stamina, and the endurance of a timber wolf. She is up to any emergency."

"And just when do you intend to desert us, may I ask?"

Unruffled, Tyler said easily, "Just as soon as I can cut my ties with Liberty Life. I changed my departure date just to have Thanksgiving with you, dear heart."

Daphne shook her head in hopeless, baffled bewilderment. "I cannot believe the evidence of my own ears!"

As if spotting a crack in Daphne's defenses, Tyler pushed on. "Have you forgotten the motto of our great state? *Qui transtulit sustinet.* He who transplants sustains."

"I haven't forgotten it, Tyler," Daphne snapped. "I never knew it. But I'm certain whoever coined the phrase was speaking of corn, not people!" She leaned toward him, studying him through narrowed, blue-tinted lids. "Tyler, I do believe you've lost your mind."

"No, Mother." Again he smiled with maddening self-assurance. "I've only just found it! For example, consider the concept of time. Do you realize that man created the concept of time, only to become a slave to it? No longer will I be regimented. My nomadic soul will be set free!"

With some asperity, Daphne said, "I know that time is a relentless taskmaster. We all long to toss our clocks out the window, cut the phone lines, let the doorbell ring. Nonetheless, we carry on!"

Tyler grinned. "I'm a born-again pioneer. I'm going

to carry on without clocks, phones, or doorbells!"

Gail felt suddenly deflated. Daphne's vehement disapproval hadn't deterred Tyler in the least. To make matters worse, they were getting nowhere. The two of them were poles apart, each convinced the other was dead wrong. The one bright spot on Gail's horizon was that Tyler's own mother was definitely on her team. Clearly, she and Daphne needed time alone to regroup, to marshal their forces.

Smiling, Gail said through clenched teeth, "Dinner is ready."

At once Daphne rose to her feet. "I'll help you serve, my dear." In sweet-sour tones she added, "Maybe all Tyler needs is food in his stomach to clear his head."

Seated at the festive, food-laden Thanksgiving dinner table, Gail bowed her head while Tyler said grace. Silently, Gail murmured her own prayer of thanksgiving, thanking the Lord for His many blessings: for home and food, for a doting mother-in-law, and for her loving, extraordinary husband, ending with the request that the Almighty guide Tyler's footsteps in the paths of righteousness—right here in Connecticut.

Gail had no doubt that Tyler enjoyed every bite of his Thanksgiving dinner, but her marvelous traditional holiday meal did not change his determination to defect. Nor did Daphne's constant diplomatic—and not so diplomatic—digs, her dour predictions, and veiled threats of disinheritance deter him. Every time Daphne would let fly one of her poisoned darts, Gail would scowl and shake her head, fretting that Daphne was doing their cause more harm than good.

With Thanksgiving over, Gail and Daphne threw all their energies into Christmas baking, stocking the freezer for the holidays. The fragrant aromas of home-baked braided breads, gingerbread men, springerle, fruitcake, fondue, and fudge wafted through the old house.

Early one Saturday morning while they were rolling out dough for sand tarts, Daphne said in nostalgic tones, "I love Christmas. Christmas in Connecticut," she went on, whirling the rolling pin over the pale, creamy dough in joyous abandon.

"So do I." With the back of her hand, Gail rubbed a smudge of flour from her nose. "It's my favorite holiday. Tyler's, too."

"This year we must make it the best Christmas ever," Daphne said. "If that doesn't convince Tyler that his roots are right here, nothing will."

Gail grinned. "We'll make it the best of all time—a Christmas Tyler will remember all the days of his life!"

Daphne's laughter rang out. "That sounds like a threat."

Gail smiled a secret smile. "Whatever's fair."

"Are you sure he'll be here for Christmas?"

"No. I'm afraid to ask. I might not like the answer. I believe in letting sleeping dogs lie."

As if having mentioned sleeping dogs had brought them to life, Gail's question was answered that same night.

Tyler burst into the house all but gnashing his teeth. For one heart-stopping moment, Gail thought he would take the next plane out of Hartford.

"What's wrong?" she cried, alarmed.

"Connecticut Liberty Life is what's wrong!" Tyler shouted. "Today they told me they've hired my replacement. But he can't start until December fifteenth." Tyler's lips tightened with exasperation. "That really ties it!"

"Ties it?" Gail echoed.

"Ties it," Tyler repeated flatly. "They went me to stay

on another month to train him. I told them I'd stay just two weeks, till December thirty-first. Then *exitus et libertas!* Up, up, and away!"

Gail nodded sympathetically. "I understand how annoying it is to have to change your plans again, Tyler. It's as if your entire future is hanging in air." But her heart was singing, *Praise the Lord!*

 *9*

A MONSTROUS SNOWSTORM CAME the first Sunday in December, clogging the roads, swirling in knee-high drifts down the lane, piling up along the picket fence. Tyler, who had been outside shoveling a path down the lane, stamped through the doorway of the keeping room looking half frozen.

Daphne regarded him with an unsympathetic eye. "Just whom do you expect to do all this shoveling after you've gone, Tyler?"

Tyler grinned. "Gail can shovel. She can do anything!"

"And what if the pipes freeze?" Daphne asked testily. "Can Gail fix those, too?"

"No, and neither can I." Tyler chuckled. "Every year we pray that the furnace goes on before the pipes freeze."

"Humph!" Daphne snorted, plainly unwilling to deny the power of prayer. "And what if the electricity goes

130

off during a sleet storm?" she persisted. "Can Gail handle that?"

"You bet," Tyler said with a confident grin. "I'll show you." He went to the hutch, opened the lower door, and brought out two glass-chimneyed oil lamps. Smiling affably, he said, "There are others strewn about the house. I'll get them. Be prepared, I always say."

The next thing Gail knew, she and Daphne were cleaning and filling them. Tyler left the room. When he returned, bearing two more lamps, Daphne said briskly, "Tyler, since you believe so strongly in being prepared, you just find yourself a rag and set about preparing!"

Amusement sparkled in his light brown eyes. "Whatever you say, Mother!" And with good-natured aplomb, he complied.

The next morning, bent on doing their Christmas shopping early, Gail and Daphne drove into the village. They passed roadside stands where great piles of Christmas trees for sale spiced the crisp, cold air with the pungent scent of pine. Daphne exclaimed delightedly over doorways decorated with wreaths or swags of fresh pine and cones, Christmas lights strung on trees and bushes, and the giant pine glowing with brightly colored lights in the village square.

As Gail and Daphne browsed slowly along the main street, enlivened by the display of crèches, glittering stars, huge electric candles, and garlanded store windows, their holiday spirits soared. They both dropped bills into a black pot manned by a smiling Santa vigorously ringing a bell, then parted to carry out mysterious errands. At noon they met for lunch at a charming eighteenth-century Colonial tearoom. Both exuded an air of excitement and carried snugly wrapped parcels whose contents would be kept secret till Christmas Day. When they had finished their lunch and were lingering over a second pot of tea, Daphne grew suddenly quiet, as if lost in silent reverie.

"Memories?" Gail asked softly.

Daphne nodded. In quiet, reflective tones, she said, "I love coming home to Connecticut. I think a person always has a special feeling for the place where he was born."

"I hope so!" Gail said fervently.

"Don't misunderstand, dear. I love my life in Phoenix, wouldn't trade it for the world. But Connecticut will always be *home*. Home is where the heart is, you know."

"I hope so, Daphne. I hope home is where Tyler's heart is . . . home in Connecticut."

"I'm sure it is, dear. Still, I must admit he can be rather pigheaded. But he's a Gemini, so what can you expect? It's his nature. Other pastures always look greener. A Gemini makes these quick decisions, then changes his mind."

Gail's lips curved in a wary smile. "Tyler doesn't appear to be changing his mind."

Daphne shook her head in vexation. "Geminis don't know what they want!" She looked at Gail inquiringly. "You're August—a Leo, right?"

Gail shook her head. "August twenty-eighth, Virgo."

"Oh, dear. Not at all harmonious with Gemini. But you do respond favorably during a crisis, and you're especially good at bringing order out of chaos."

"Maybe," said Gail ruefully. "But this is *Tyler's* chaos."

"True." Daphne paused, as if sorting out her thoughts. "Do you know what I think? I think Tyler's going through an early midlife crisis. His dear father was the same way.

The years fly by. Thirty-five sneaks up on them, passes them before they know it. Forty looming on the horizon makes them terribly edgy. I'm afraid Tyler is simply running the other way."

Gail sat very straight in her chair and squared her shoulders. "If he's suffering a midlife crisis, we'll have to see him through it."

Daphne appeared to be studying the leaves in the bottom of her teacup. "I just hope you won't get discouraged and give up. Perhaps you can think of a way to slow down his midlife crisis—or a way to hurry it up, so things can get back to normal."

Thoughts whirred like windmills in Gail's mind. Just thinking about ways she could help Tyler cope with his midlife crisis made her clear gray eyes turn to pools of pure love. She smiled into Daphne's eyes. "Don't worry, Daphne. I'm tough and strong, and I'll never give up."

The following week Gail and Daphne set about decorating the house. They hung a pine wreath bright with red berries on the front door and framed the doorway in fresh green pine. They swathed the mantels with garlands of greens and red velvet bows and tall red candles. Gail stuck sprigs of juniper in with the bittersweet in the brass bowl, and Daphne bought six poinsettias, whose scarlet blooms gave the sunroom a festive air. On a wide windowsill in the keeping room, Tyler set up a crèche, an ancient manger scene that had once belonged to Daphne's grandmother.

Gail saw Daphne watching him. Her mother-in-law's nose turned suddenly pink, her eyes suspiciously moist.

Softly, Daphne said, "I always hoped that someday I would see my grandchildren set up this crèche."

Gail flung her arms around her shoulders. "Don't give up too soon, Daphne. Where there's life, there's hope."

"Whoever said that doesn't know Tyler Peabody," Daphne said flatly.

Tyler chuckled. "You can hardly expect him to! John Gay said it in the 1700s in *The Sick Man and the Angel*."

"Humph!" Daphne said, then spoke no more.

One week before Christmas, Tyler struggled through the back door proudly clutching a fresh, fragrant, perfectly shaped Frasier fir tree. "Prettiest tree we've ever had!" Daphne exclaimed. "And the best smelling!" Gail added, happily sniffing the sharp, tangy boughs.

Tyler set up the tree in a corner of the keeping room, and on Christmas Eve, Gail, Daphne, and Tyler trimmed it. As was his custom, Tyler stood on a small step ladder and with great care began stringing the big old-fashioned lights that had once belonged to Daphne's mother.

As she did every year, Gail asked, "Why don't you plug in the lights to see if they work before you string them on the tree?"

And as he did every year, Tyler, carried away by his enthusiasm, shook his head and went on happily stringing.

Smiling to herself, Gail shook her head. Dear, obstinate Tyler never would test the waters before taking the plunge. A troubled frown creased her brow, as the thought came to her that he was plunging into the waters of Tahiti in the same way. A sudden flash of light distracted her. One string of lights shone with brilliant glowing colors; the other remained dark. An omen? Gail wondered with a slight chill. Now, as always, Tyler swore under his breath, found fresh bulbs, and set about replacing the culprits. At last he flung up his arms and shouted, "Let there be light!" He thrust the plug in the socket and the dark string burst into bloom.

With great care, Gail and Daphne unwrapped bright, shiny ornaments, fragile family heirlooms shaped like fruits, or balls, or birds of paradise with silk tails. Tyler put a tape of Christmas carols on the cassette deck, and Gail, in a burst of goodwill and optimism, hummed loudly along with the carolers, "Oh, come, all ye faithful!" Surely, she thought, carrying out their most treasured family traditions, Tyler would see that here was where he belonged, that he could find his real self right in his own backyard!

When they had hung the last glistening ornament on the tree, they brought their gifts from their secret hiding places and set them under the spreading branches of the brightly decorated evergreen. Curiosity gleamed in Tyler's eyes. "There sure are some mysterious and intriguing-looking shapes and sizes in that pile of packages! How about giving me just a hint..."

"No way!" Gail grinned. She had found the absolutely perfect gift for Tyler. Not only would it be a surprise, but it would be a challenge as well. The very thing to keep him at home! A sudden silence fell upon them. As if by common consent, they stood back to gaze with pleasure and admiration at the rich, dark green glowing tree.

Daphne let out a long, happy sigh. "I love being with you dears, especially at Christmas. I wouldn't miss being here for all the world!" She leveled a hard, expectant gaze on Tyler.

Gail thought she may just as well have said, "Would

you, Tyler?," for her unspoken question hung in the air. Daphne continued to stare at Tyler, silently demanding an answer.

His warm brown eyes met hers, and his face lighted with a gentle smile. "I'm glad you wouldn't miss being here, dear heart, because we love having you."

On Christmas morning Gail awoke shortly after dawn. Glancing at the window, she smiled in delight. During the night, it had snowed, draping each small pane with white velvet. She jumped out of bed and ran to close the window. Shivering, she breathed deeply of the sharp, crystalline air and gazed with pleasure over the white landscape spread before her, so silent it seemed she and Tyler were the only people in the world. Joy and excitement coursed through her. There was something very special about this day, like no other in all the year. And this Christmas day would be more special, different from all the others. Her heart swelled with anticipation and dread. This could be the last Christmas she and Tyler would ever spend together. Or, it could herald a turning point in their lives—the day Tyler decided *not* to make his Great Escape...that there was no place like home. Which would it be? Excitement tingled through her.

Swiftly, she crossed to the bed and shook Tyler by the shoulder. "Merry Christmas, love!" She dropped a light butterfly kiss on each eyelid. "Wake up, darling."

"Uh," Tyler grunted. "What time is it?"

"Time to get up! Come on, hurry! I can hardly wait to give you your gifts!"

He rolled over and locked his arms around Gail's waist, pulling her down on the bed. His hand slid up her back, pressing her close to his chest. He buried his face in her hair, nuzzling her ear. In deep, drowsy, sensuous tones, he murmured, "You can give me a gift right now, and then we'll drift and dream for a while. It's indecent to get up this early on a holiday."

Feigning indignation, Gail warned sternly, "Tyler, you're forgetting again! Forgetting to deny yourself!"

Tyler bit her earlobe gently. "You can't expect me to deny myself on Christmas Day." In noble, generous tones, he added, "I certainly don't expect you to!" He curved a hand around her bottom and pulled her closer against him. His free hand stroked her cheek, strayed down her neck, fondling her throat and breast. Eagerly, his lips closed over hers.

She could feel her body responding to his touch. A delicious shiver swept through her. It was warm and cozy lying in Tyler's arms in an intimate embrace here in their cocoon of quilts. She was terribly tempted. It would be fun, snuggling, making love, starting the day with morning delight. But she mustn't let herself be sidetracked!

Laughing, she turned her head aside and wriggled from his grasp. The instant her feet touched the cold, polished pine floor, she caught up the quilts and flung them to the foot of the bed. "Come on, Tyler. No more shilly-shallying. Hit the deck!" Gail slipped into her burgundy *panné* velvet robe and slippers, then picked up her hairbrush and began to stroke the long, shining strands.

"Hey!" Tyler howled. "It's cold in here!" He sat up abruptly and lunged for the quilts at the foot of the bed.

"Right!" Grinning wickedly, Gail snatched the quilts from Tyler's grasp, dumped them in the dower chest, and slammed the lid. "Better hurry downstairs to see what Santa brought you."

Through teeth that chattered violently, and, Gail

thought, intentionally and unnecessarily loudly, Tyler said, "M-m-m-maybe he's br-r-brought me some c-c-coal!"

"Probably," she agreed cheerily. "It's no less than you deserve."

Tyler's brows rose in disdain. "I mean, coal to feed the furnace."

Gail chuckled. "Whatever's fair! But you'll never know if you don't get a move on. So hurry! I'm going to wake Daphne, then start breakfast."

As Gail had hoped, the heady fragrance of coffee perking and the heavenly aroma of pancakes cooking brought both Daphne and Tyler to the table fast. They wolfed down their breakfast as if there were no tomorrow—because it tasted so good, they said.

The corners of Gail's lips quirked in amusement. "Gobbling down your food has nothing to do with the presents waiting under the tree. Right?"

"Of course not!" Tyler pushed back his chair and rose to his feet. "But we don't want to keep them waiting."

Eagerly, they gathered around the tree. To Gail, the colorful twinkling lights and shiny ornaments seemed to glow with promise. She sprawled on the braided rug beside Sidney. Daphne perched on a footstool waiting for Tyler to hand out the gifts. He hunkered down and picked up one from the pile spread under the tree. He read the card aloud. "Merry Christmas to Daphne, with love from Sidney Peabody."

"My, how neatly it's wrapped," Daphne said, carefully undoing the paper. "Oh, how nice!" she exclaimed, holding up a plastic bag full of tennis balls. "How thoughtful of Sidney!"

Gail smiled. "Sidney picked those out himself, mostly in the roads on our walks around the village. He especially likes those bilious green ones."

Daphne patted Sidney on the head. "So do I, so do I!"

There was a skirt for Daphne as well, and a tan leather carrying bag for her golf clubs. Sidney gave Tyler a miniature rosebush to be grown indoors, and Daphne gave Tyler a thick book with handsome color photographs entitled *Connecticut, the Best of Everything. Be There!* For Gail, Daphne had found a new book of quilt patterns. Fur-lined gloves for Gail came from J. Alfred Prufrock, and from Sidney, a huge bottle of *Toujours Moi*.

Gail reached down and scratched Sidney's ears. "Don't worry, Sid. With me, it's always 'Always You'!"

Tyler presented Sidney with a monstrous box of dog bones, and gave J. Alfred Prufrock a colorful porcelain castle with myriad exits and entrances. "I thought he needed new pathways to swim, to spice up his life," Tyler explained unnecessarily. Gail's mouth turned down at the corners. Undaunted, Tyler gave Daphne a road atlas and a map light with a magnifying lens.

"Darling, this is wonderful! When I leave here, I'm going to spend the rest of the winter doing Texas, from Galveston to Amarillo, and Amarillo to Big Bend!"

"With this, you can drive anywhere all over the U.S., Canada, and Mexico—without getting lost!" Tyler said, plainly proud of his present.

Gail's eyes narrowed. "My, what lovely gifts! Thoughtful, too," she added, with only a hint of irony. She did not care at all for Tyler's talk of travel.

Tyler opened Gail's gift to Sidney, a brass name tag for his collar that read: SIDNEY THE WONDER DOG, along with his license and phone number.

Clearly, Tyler was saving his main gift to Gail, and

hers to him, to open till last. And, finally, all the other gifts were gone. Suspense had been building inside her all morning long. Unable to endure waiting another second, Gail burst out, "Tyler, for heaven's sake, open your gift from me!"

To make sure it was a surprise, to disguise its shape to keep him from guessing what it was, she had wrapped it in a big oblong box. Slowly, carefully, with maddening deliberation, Tyler slid the crimson ribbon off the ends of the box and tugged at the tape sealing the gold-foil paper.

"I bet it's a suitcase," Daphne bubbled cheerily. "You can never have enough luggage, going off *forever!*" She stressed the word "forever" in tones of sharp disapproval.

Gail shot her a dark, savage look. She leaned close to Daphne and under cover of the rustling paper whispered, "Don't even *think* 'forever'!"

Tyler's face glowed with anticipation. "I think it's some sort of trunk, one of those old brass-bound, bow-lidded chests to keep buried treasure in."

"You have to find it first," Daphne said crisply. "And where your treasure is, there your heart lies also."

Tyler's brown eyes sparkled with mirth, as if in amused indulgence at his mother's jibes about going away. "I told you, I'm not searching for treasure, I'm searching for the real me."

Gail could stand the suspense no longer. "Just get on with it, Tyler."

Grinning, he stripped off the paper, eased off the lid, and lifted Gail's gift from the box. He held it by the neck with one hand, away from his body. He stood staring at it, as though suddenly struck dumb. In the awed silence, the radiators hissed and bubbled, the clock struck the quarter hour, and the windows rattled. In quick succession, expressions of wonder, astonishment, and bewilderment flashed across Tyler's face. At last he turned toward Gail, regarding her with a faint, quizzical smile.

"Gail, darling, this is a beautiful gift. I really appreciate it. But I don't know how to play a ukulele."

"I *know* that, Tyler. That's one reason I gave it to you. Learning to play it will give you something to do on your desert island, or if you *should* change your mind about Tahiti, on the sun-baked sands of the Sahara, or in your sheepherder's wagon in Wyoming." She smiled appealingly into his eyes. "You could even learn to play it right here in Connecticut."

"And then you could teach me, Tyler!" Daphne said, bubbling with enthusiasm. "I'd love to go to Hawaii and play the ukulele. Everyone in the Hawaiian islands plays the ukulele. It's so romantic." An ecstatic sigh escaped her, and a dreamy, otherworldly look came into her eyes. "Who knows, one day I may even play my own 'Hawaiian Wedding Song'!"

Gail gritted her teeth and gazed heavenward, thinking, Daphne's as bad as Tyler, indulging in fantasies. It must be in their genes!

Tyler leaned over and gave his mother a peck on the cheek. "That wouldn't surprise me one bit! Hang on to your dream, dear heart. It's not at all impossible!"

He turned back to the tree and picked up the last gift, a big square box, beautifully wrapped in shiny white paper and tied with a huge gold bow. With a flourish, he thrust it into Gail's arms. "For you, my love, from me."

With shaking fingers, Gail pulled off the bow and stripped off the paper. Dumbstruck, she gazed down at the box in her lap for a long moment. She looked up at Tyler. Her lower lip quivered. Tears stung her eyelids.

"Tyler, I'm touched. Really touched!"

Tyler beamed with pleasure. "I thought you'd like it, thought it was about time we had one. Even though *I* won't be here to enjoy it, I know *you'll* love it. And, more important, it will keep you warm all winter long."

"Oh, Tyler!" Gail cried in a voice trembling with emotion. "An electric blanket can never replace you, never!"

Tyler nodded understandingly. "I know, darling. But it's better than a stick in the eye."

Gail managed a tremulous smile and made no reply. This was the end, this lovely, vile, Pepto-Bismol-pink electric blanket. It proved, once and for all, that Tyler had no intention of changing his mind. He really *was* going to leave her!

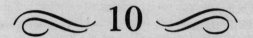

10

TWO DAYS LATER, on the eve of Daphne's departure, Gail went to her room to help her pack her bags. Once again, they hashed over the problem of Tyler's Great Escape.

Sorrowfully, Daphne said, "My dear, at first I could only regard Tyler's irresponsible decision with stunned disbelief. But now"—she gave a hopeless shake of her wavy blond head—"I'm convinced that nothing will deter him. I've done my best these past weeks, pointed out the folly of his decision at every turn, but the scoundrel simply tunes me out. I'm afraid he actually intends to desert us. I'm sorry to say, I've done all I can do. I must get on with my life. I must be on the road again." A bubbling, apologetic laugh escaped her. "So much to see—and I have to get your money's worth from your wonderful atlas. I go reluctantly, and with great misgivings, Gail, dear, for it's plain to see that Tyler isn't even halfway through his midlife crisis. I'm afraid all is lost!"

Gail took a deep breath to bolster her courage. She couldn't let Daphne down. She couldn't let *herself* down. She stiffened her spine and, with steely-eyed determination, lifted her chin like a soldier going into battle. "Don't worry, Daphne. I'll muddle through."

But when Daphne left the next morning, all Gail's hopes of keeping Tyler at home went with her.

All day long, Gail felt as though she had lost her last friend and ally. Bereft, she wandered through the house, in and out of each room, sensing its emptiness. Sidney, as though sensing her despondent mood, her feeling of abandonment, followed close on her heels.

She shivered. "I feel invisible, Sidney, like a ghost left on duty to haunt the place." At length she wandered back to the keeping room and sank down in her chair, staring with unseeing eyes out the window. Sidney sat on his haunches before her and put his head in her lap. Nudging her hands with his cold, wet nose, he gazed up into her face with a sad, injured air, as if to say, "Don't despair, you still have me!"

Gail smiled wryly. "I know, Sidney. I still have you. And you are still my best friend." With renewed determination, she rose from her chair, dragged herself upstairs to her studio, and attacked Tyler's bust.

Today, even her studio seemed dark and gloomy. She glanced out the window at the sky, like dull pewter, looking as if a blizzard were on the way. The juncos were huddled on tree limbs, their feathers bunched against the bitter cold. Not a creature stirred in the meadow. Her dark mood brightened. Maybe there would be a blizzard like the blizzard of 1960, the granddaddy of all snowstorms, with seventeen inches of snow in one day, the next day more snow, and the next day, snow and sleet. It had paralyzed the village for days. Even Tyler couldn't escape in such a blizzard! The prospect cheered her only briefly, for knowing Tyler, she figured he would find a way. She brooded all day long. By the time Tyler walked through the door that evening, her mood was as black and ominous as the dark clouds looming overhead.

To make matters worse, Tyler's face, red with cold, was wreathed in smiles. He could not have been more high-spirited if he'd dived down a rabbit hole and found himself in Tahiti. Gail turned back to the stove and, with unusual vigor, stirred the cheese melting for their Welsh rarebit.

Tyler strode to her side. Parting the fall of her thick, curling, glossy black hair, he planted a crisp, cold kiss on the back of her neck, then gave her a friendly pat on the bottom, chatting animatedly all the while. If he noticed her lack of response, he showed no sign of it. He took off his hat, coat, and scarf and flung them on the hall tree.

"It's starting to snow," Tyler remarked with cheerful goodwill. "Dry, tight, swirling flakes."

Gail pursed her lips, scowling. That he was taking it with such good grace was a bad omen. Usually, he growled his displeasure over the least sign of a snowstorm.

"Hmm," Gail said. Her voice rose on a note of optimism. "Maybe we'll have another blizzard, like the one in 1960. *The Old Farmer's Almanac* says it was the worst on record. It started just like this," she went on happily, "with dry, swirling snow, ending with snow and sleet. Pipes froze, electricity went off, even the snowplows couldn't get through. Nothing moved for days."

Tyler patted Sidney's head, crossed to J. Alfred Prufrock's bowl, and shook in a little fish food. Not the least bit perturbed, he remarked casually, pleasantly, "If we're going to have a blizzard, I hope it's now, so it'll be over with before I take off."

Gail's hand seemed to freeze on the handle of the spoon. She didn't care to hear talk of taking off.

Without waiting for her reply, Tyler rattled on. "Miss Curtis called me today. My passport came. I'm to stop by and pick it up. She'll make my plane reservations, and I'll be ready to roll!"

A sharp, searing pain seemed to knife through Gail's breast. She bit her lip to keep from crying out. Holding herself tightly under control, she said evenly, "Tyler, you absolutely cannot leave now. I haven't finished your bust, and you haven't learned to play your ukulele."

Tyler smiled fatuously at J. Alfred Prufrock, tailing him through the water with one finger. In jovial tones, he said, "I can delay no longer, my love. Go, I must." He crossed to *The Old Farmer's Almanac* lying on the counter, and flipped it open. "I want to check out the weather forecast so I can plan to leave when the signs are right."

Gail made no reply, but dished up the Welsh rarebit and set their plates on the table along with spinach salad, baked stuffed mushrooms, and corn muffins. Dazedly, she sat down at the table. Love and heartbreak and anger were all roiling around inside her.

Tyler slid into his chair across from her. He leveled an appraising gaze on her face, as if trying to read her thoughts. Finally, he said quietly, "Gail, love, I thought we might have sort of a small celebration on Monday night—go out for dinner, a show..."

Gail raised her eyes to meet his. "Why?"

Tyler gave a slight shrug of his shoulders. "Well, for one thing, it's New Year's Eve. More important, Monday will be my last day with Connecticut Liberty Life..."

A startled, surprised expression flashed into her eyes.

"Oh, Tyler. I'm sorry. I'm afraid I just blocked out your last day at work. It isn't a thing I like to think about."

In dry tones that held a hint of reproach, he went on: "Usually, when a man retires from work, he receives some recognition. Today the president and three V.P.'s took me out to lunch. And, as a token of the company's esteem, they gave me a gold pen and pencil set." A wry smile tugged at the corners of his mouth.

Watching him, Gail couldn't tell whether he was pleased with Liberty Life's parting gesture, or merely pleased to be leaving. With hearty enthusiasm, she said, "That's great, Tyler, really great." But even to her own ears, her words sounded false. *She* wasn't pleased that he was leaving, and for the life of her, she couldn't see how Tyler could use a gold pen and pencil set in Tahiti.

"On Monday I'll be given my ten-year bonus, along with a fat severance check." His eyes glowed with an unholy light, as if envisioning a wondrous future. He gazed at Gail expectantly. "In my book, retiring is cause for celebration."

Gail felt something green and unlovely uncoiling inside her. In sugar-coated tones, she said, "You're too young to retire, Tyler. In your case, it's called quitting."

A deep red flush crept up Tyler's neck, suffusing his face. "Call it what you will; the bottom line is *the end.*"

The terrible fear that had roiled about inside her all day long suddenly sprang to life. It was actually happening. Something exploded inside her. She set down her knife and fork and stared at Tyler straight in the eye.

In the loud, stern, decisive tones used by the heads of boards of directors, Gail said, "Tyler, I've stood all of this nonsense I intend to. If that's what you want, fine. Go, and Godspeed!" Without knowing she was going to say them, words continued to pour out. "I'm tired of our structured, regimented life too. And I'm tired of keeping up this huge old house." She raised her arm in a sweeping gesture. "And I'm fed up with all these old antiques. I've decided to move to a new, modern condo."

Tyler gasped, his eyes bulging in astonishment. Gail found his thunderstruck expression and startled gasp very gratifying.

At last Tyler found his voice. "Are you sure you're not fed up with your old, antique husband?"

She gave him a fond smile. "Never that, Tyler. Anyway, you're a mere stripling as far as being an antique goes. Still, you are becoming more handsome and more valuable every year, with that marvelous patina of age." She thought she saw him wince and quickly tried to make amends. "But without you," she said brokenly, "this house and all our fine furniture mean nothing. Nothing! You must see that I can't endure living here without you." She paused, waiting for his assent, but his eyes appeared glazed, his tongue seemed stuck to the roof of his mouth. She rushed on: "So we need to start making plans right away. I'll keep Sidney with me, of course, and you can take J. Alfred Prufrock."

"No way!" Tyler bellowed. "*I* will take Sidney. A man and his dog are as inseparable as Siamese twins."

"It is possible to have surgery to remedy that, my love. But I doubt it will be necessary, because you won't be allowed to bring a dog into a foreign country." Gail cast a reassuring glance at Sidney, who was resting in his basket, seeming to stare through his black spectacles at Gail and Tyler with stern disapproval.

Tyler's features contorted in an unpleasant scowl. "That's in England. And you can bring dogs into England after a six-month quarantine."

"But you're not going to England."

"I *know!*" Tyler shouted. "That's what I'm trying to tell you. I can take Sidney to Tahiti."

Gail lifted her chin in a lofty tilt. "What is the source of your information? Do you know that for a fact?"

Tyler looked sheepish. "Well, no, but I'm positive I can take Sidney with me."

"And I say you can't!"

"What is the source of *your* information?"

She had hoped he wouldn't ask, because her research for her South Seas island supper hadn't covered importation of dogs. Defiantly, she said, "*I* am the source of my information. Even if the king of Tahiti says you can bring Sidney, I say you can't. Besides, I need him to pull the sled."

"We'll see about that!" Tyler snapped.

"Listen, Tyler, if you want to get involved in a custody battle, it's okay with me, but you might miss your flight."

"The hell I will!"

Gail narrowed her eyes, and picking up her knife, she pointed it threateningly across the table. "You're not going to take that dog one step out of the state of Connecticut!"

At the sound of the words "dog" and "out," Sidney leaped to his feet and danced around the table.

Tyler roared, "Lie down, Sidney, and shut up!"

"Stop shouting at Sidney!" Gail thundered. Privately, she was overjoyed. Tyler was getting really upset. She was finally getting through to him. It was a heady experience, and she was loving every minute of it. Boldly, she went on: "You see that? You're not a fit person to have custody of a dog. If you want to take a companion on this odyssey, you can take J. Alfred Prufrock!"

Tyler fairly screeched. "Alfred Prufrock!"

"*J*. Alfred Prufrock," Gail said primly. "That *is* his name, isn't it?" As an afterthought, she said, "You may have to get a passport for him."

Tyler's chin jutted forward. He leaned across the table, and biting off each word like the head of a nail, he spat them out: "That is absolutely, without a doubt, the most inane statement I have ever heard!"

Gail's eyes widened in innocent astonishment. "Why, Tyler, how can you say that? I'm certain J.A. would like nothing better than to float around those coral reefs in those warm, azure waters with exotic angel fish, blue tails, and tigers. He'd cut quite a swath among them, I'm sure."

"J.A. is not going to cut a swath anywhere but right here in his glass bowl," Tyler said flatly.

Gail smiled and gave a helpless shrug of her shoulders. "Too bad for J.A. then, because there won't be anyone here to watch him cutting his swath. The day you go, I go."

Tyler looked incredulous. "You mean you'd desert that poor, helpless fish?"

Gail shrugged again. "Okay, Tyler. I'll leave the day *before* you do. Last one out is the deserter. I'll be the desertee."

Tyler's voice turned persuasive, exaggeratedly patient, reasonable. "Gail, why won't you keep him?"

Gail eyed him sternly. "This may come as a great shock to you, Tyler, but I have never liked J. Alfred Prufrock. He is arrogant, superior, a showoff, the way he fishtails around in that flashy way. Besides, he's gotten too big for his bowl. He is your pet. I refuse to assume responsibility for him, and I'm through discussing the matter."

They finished their meal in silence. And through the long evening, they sat in the keeping room in silence. Gail, feeling utterly devastated, could think of nothing to say. She knew Tyler was dying to talk about winging off to Tahiti, and that was the last thing she wanted to talk about.

Once, he looked up from his paper and said in casual tones, "Gail, about the house. This is your house as well as mine, and, well, you've always said how much you love it . . ."—he took a deep breath—". . . and I just don't see how you can walk off and leave it."

"I can walk off and leave something I love exactly the way you can, Tyler."

"But with me, it's different. I'm searching for the real me. You've found your niche, right here."

She shot him a sad, wistful smile. "I'm looking for a new niche. And what I really can't stand is talking about it."

Tyler, looking miffed, picked up his brochures, then began leafing through them. Gail bit her tongue.

It wasn't until after they had gone upstairs and had climbed into bed that Tyler tried once again to smooth things over. Gail lay on her side, facing away from him, feeling miserable. He rolled over and curved his long, lean body around hers, spoon fashion, pressing his warm chest against her shoulders, his knees against her bottom, entwining his feet with hers. His breath, sweet as apples, was warm on her neck. His lips brushed her ear, sending tiny ripples tingling down her spine.

"Gail, love, we've never gone to sleep with an argument unsettled. We can't start now, just when I'm leaving."

Softly, she murmured, "Maybe you'd better stay."

As if he hadn't heard her, he said, "Listen, I'm sorry I got upset about the house, but really, Gail, it shouldn't be left standing empty."

She felt his hand on her shoulder, caressing, sliding down her arm, down hip and thigh. She moved away from him. His hand moved with her, traveling upward. She reveled in the firm touch of his fingers circling her hipbone, across her abdomen, stroking downward. A little thrill of desire fluttered through her.

She grabbed his hand and held it snugly at her waist. "You're right, love. I guess you'll have to rent it out."

She felt his body stiffen against her own. "Rent it out! Rent our house to perfect strangers?"

She rubbed her cold feet against his warm, hairy shins. "Unless you can rent it to someone we know."

He disengaged his hand from hers and curving it under her chin turned her head to face him. In the glow of the flickering firelight, he gazed deeply into her eyes.

"Gail, truthfully now, would you really want to let someone else live in our house?"

"No," she said softly. "I wouldn't. I guess we'll have to sell it. Then it will be someone else's house."

His hand strayed downward and curved around her left breast, warm and loving. "Darling, you're being deliberately difficult." Before she could reply, his mouth found hers. Tyler's nimble fingers freed the buttons at the neck of Gail's red flannel gown. Time passed, punctuated by countless, blissful moments of delight.

When at last Gail caught her breath, she asked, "What do you mean, I'm being difficult? I think I'm being very cooperative."

"Mmm," Tyler said, easing her onto her back and kissing each breast in turn, again and again.

Gail arched her back, moving sensuously under his

tender assault in a feeble effort to escape. She must remind Tyler to deny himself. She gripped his shoulders, the better to push him away. "Tyler," she murmured, "we've both forgotten something." Then, to her own astonishment, instead of pushing Tyler away, her hands, seemingly of their own volition, pulled him closer and closer, cheek to cheek, heart to heart, hip to hip, thigh to thigh.

"Oh?" Tyler muttered. His lips explored the hollow between her breasts. "What have we forgotten?"

Dreamily, lost in the rapture of Tyler's embrace, so welcome after enduring the endless torture of days and nights of doing without, Gail struggled to speak. With her last crumb of willpower, she dredged up an answer.

"I forget."

Some little time later, when their passions were at last sated and Gail felt as though she were floating free in space, orbiting the moon, she heard Tyler's far distant voice.

"Then you *will* stay in the house while I'm gone, won't you, darling?"

Her euphoria began to fade. A regretful sigh escaped her.

"Whatever's fair, my love, whatever's fair."

She smiled to herself, thinking: Tyler knows as well as anyone that all is fair in love and war. She had given him a final taste of the joys of marital bliss that he would be giving up; given him a clear warning that he could not leave his house and have it, too. The chips were down. She had called his bluff. And she was sure she held the winning hand.

~ 11 ~

THE NEXT MORNING Gail awakened to the sound of a dull roar outside, like a furious lion, which she recognized as the snowplow trundling down the road. She scowled in annoyance. She had looked forward greatly to being snowed in with Tyler, lazing before a cozy fire all day long.

"Cheer up!" she told herself. "Maybe all isn't lost. Maybe it snowed all night, and the lane from the barn to the road will be knee-deep in snowdrifts."

Without warning, Tyler leaped from the bed and flung on his blue velour robe. He peered out the window. "Good grief! We'll never get the car out!"

"But, Tyler, we don't need to get the car out!"

"I want to be sure I can get out tomorrow to go to work. It's my last day, remember, and I'm not going to miss it!"

Gail nodded unhappily. "How could I forget?"

"Besides, what if there's an emergency? I like to know

I can get in the car and go if I need to."

The truth is, thought Gail, the man can't bear to be snowed in, held captive, even by a blizzard!

Tyler crossed the room, entwined his fingers in Gail's hair and gently hauled her out of bed.

"Come on, woman, rustle me up some victuals."

Gail laughed. "Johnny cakes coming right up!"

A few minutes later, he gulped down his breakfast, then bolted out the door. Gail stood at the window watching him—a stalwart figure in a Loden-green jacket and red cap silhouetted against the vast white landscape— shoveling a path to the old red barn as if a thousand devils were after him.

When she heard the VW churn down the lane, she smiled to herself, thinking: Dear Tyler, always going the last mile! Has to prove to himself he can get through to the road! Several minutes passed but she didn't hear the VW churning back up the lane. She ran to the window and peered out. Her heart gave an odd lurch. The VW was gone. Sidney, too, was gone. Strange, she thought. Very strange. At once she reassured herself. Maybe Tyler had gone to fill the gas tank.

Time dragged on. Restlessly, Gail paced the parlor floor, first staring out the front windows down the road, then out the side window, watching the lane. Maybe the VW was stuck in the snow; or maybe the snowplow had plowed the old bug under. A blessing in disguise, she thought cheerfully. Just then she heard the familiar "vroom" of the engine charging across the silent, snow-laden countryside.

Moments later Tyler burst through the doorway, stamping snow from his boots, grinning from ear to ear. His eyes sparkled with joy. In triumphant tones, he shouted, "I've got it!"

"Got what?"

"My passport! And Miss Curtis and I have lined up all my reservations!" He grabbed Gail around the waist and swung her off her feet, whirling her about the room. "I leave on the fourteenth, the second Monday in January. Miss Curtis wondered if I could be ready that soon. I told her I'd been ready for weeks!" He set Gail down with a thud. "What do you think of that!"

With a numbed heart, she said weakly, "I wouldn't think the agency would be open today."

"It's always open on Sunday, remember? Miss Curtis does a lot of business on Sundays, especially on a day like this, when everybody would rather be somewhere else."

"*I* wouldn't rather be somewhere else, Tyler."

"And thank God you won't!" In a burst of joy and exuberance, he pulled Gail to him and, wrapping his arms about her, kissed her full on the lips. "I'm forever grateful to you, love. I couldn't enjoy myself for a single minute knowing this house was empty and you were stuck away in a condo!"

Gail looked deeply into his eyes, smiling wistfully. "I know, my love, I know." Quickly, she lowered her gaze. She should tell him now, but she couldn't bear to deflate his bubble of happiness. She caught her lower lip between her teeth. Now was definitely not the right time to tell him how wrong he was. She must wait for the right moment.

All day Monday Tyler was finishing up at work. That night, to celebrate New Year's Eve, they went to a nearby dinner theater; and when they got home, they welcomed in the new year with a private celebration, feasting on champagne and oysters in their four-poster bed.

New Year's Day, which Gail wanted to keep festive, was certainly no time to bring up anything controversial. Nor did the right moment present itself on Wednesday, Thursday, or Friday, for Tyler was hurrying around in a distraught way, buying khaki shorts and a bush jacket, and a zoom lens and film for his camera. There was little Gail could do to help, for Tyler had definite ideas about what to take and how to pack. However, she did pack his lavalava and insisted he take a year's supply of vitamins and get a smallpox shot. Gail busied herself in the barn, out of harm's way, telling Tyler she was getting things organized before his departure. He was always a little tense when packing for a long trip, and on Friday night he had a trial packing run.

"I know I don't have to pack for another week," he explained, "but I have to make sure I can get everything in." He packed and repacked all his worldly goods that he couldn't live without. "It's the books that are causing the problem," Tyler said, visibly agitated.

"Don't worry, love," Gail reassured him. "Just pack everything else and I'll ship all your books to you in a big carton, air express."

Reluctantly, Tyler set about repacking everything but his books. It was after midnight when he finished, tired and disgruntled. Almost, thought Gail, bordering on bearish. Now was certainly not the right moment to tell him. The truth was, she hated to tell Tyler anything that might make him unhappy during their last days together. But now she was down to the wire. There was nothing for it. "I'll tell him tomorrow," she promised herself aloud, "first thing in the morning."

Morning came too soon, accompanied by the sound

of vigorous pounding on the front door and excited voices spiraling upward through their bedroom window. Gail's eyes flew open.

As though shot from a cannon, Tyler jerked bolt upright, looking frantically around the room. "What's that? What's all that racket?"

Gail smiled faintly, trying to appear as ignorant as Tyler of what was going on while racking her brain trying to think of what to say. She heard a car chugging up the lane. Tyler leaped out of bed, flung a quilt around his shoulders, and dashed to the window.

"Good Lord. There's a damned parade out there! People milling around our house, and cars turning in, driving right up our lane."

Gail swallowed hard, squirming under the quilt.

Tyler swung to face her. "Come here, quick!" he shouted. "Look at all those people! Can you believe this?"

Gail slid out of bed and went to stand beside Tyler at the window. In sober tones, she said, "I can believe it."

Tyler eyed her with a puzzled, curious gaze. "You don't seem surprised."

Gail gazed fixedly over the heads of the crowd below into the distance. "I'm not surprised."

A spark of suspicion kindled and grew in Tyler's clear brown eyes. "Gail, do you know who those people are—what they're doing here at seven-thirty on Saturday morning?"

Gail caught her lip between her teeth. If she answered Tyler's question, all hell would break loose. Mutely, she nodded.

Tyler grabbed her shoulders and gave her a frantic shake. His voice rose, loud, excited, demanding.

"Gail, who are those people?"

"I think they've come for the yard sale."

"Yard sale!" he screeched. *"What* yard sale?"

Gail's lips curved in an implacable smile. "Our yard sale. I put an ad in the paper."

"Ad in the paper!" Tyler bellowed.

Tartly, Gail asked, "Why do you keep repeating everything I say? What are you, a parrot?"

"Don't try to change the subject!" Tyler shouted.

Quietly, she said, "I'm not deaf, Tyler. You don't have to shout."

"I'm not shouting!" he shouted. "I'm just trying to find out what the hell's going on in my own yard!"

The clamor below grew louder. Someone pounded on the door. Gail leaned out the window. "Hang in there, folks. The sale doesn't start till eight o'clock." She slammed the window down. "Goodness. I'd better get down there right now!"

Tyler, looking flushed and upset, said flatly, "And I am going right back to bed. I am *not* taking part in any yard sale to unload all our old junk." Defiantly, he flung himself onto the bed.

Strangely, the more excited Tyler grew, the calmer Gail felt. Softly, she replied, "I know you're not taking part in the yard sale, Tyler. *I* am." Hurriedly, she began to dress. Tyler sat on the bed watching her, mouth agape, as if she'd suddenly sprouted horns and a tail.

Pulling on a yellow sweat shirt and jeans, she said cheerfully, "I *am* surprised that there's such a big crowd. I guess what hooked them was the magic word in the ad."

Tyler cocked his head, fixing her with a curious stare. "Oh, what was that?"

She paused in the doorway and glanced back over her shoulder, grinning. "Antiques!"

"Antiques!" Tyler exploded. "If you think I'm going to stand by and let you sell..."

She went out, closing the door softly behind her.

She hurried across the yard toward the barn, thinking she couldn't have asked for a better day. The rising sun tinted the snowy ground with a golden, rosy light, striking crystal fire. She breathed deeply of the sharp wintry air, letting it out in small cloud puffs. As she crossed the yard, several of the villagers called out a greeting. The cheerful, chattering crowd exuded on air of anticipation and excitement at the prospect of finding a treasure, a bargain in a barn full of antiques.

The sun spilled its warmth over the glittering white-quilted yard, melting the snow on the gravel turnaround. Struck by an inspiration, Gail turned and ran back inside the house. One by one, she carried several choice pieces of furniture outside to tempt prospective buyers. That done, she invaded the barn.

She took up a pitchfork, broke open one of the bales of hay stacked in one corner, then spread it around the floor to add a bit of warmth underfoot. At eight o'clock on the dot, she opened the barn doors. Avid bargain hunters streamed inside. With some difficulty, Gail dragged a pedestal table and four Hitchcock chairs through the crowd to add to her outdoor display. She was tugging on one end of a dower chest when a stocky, bearded man in his forties, wearing a gray Astrakhan hat and a long black coat, picked up the other end. Together, they hauled it outside. They had carted out six barley wheat chairs, three nightstands, and a small walnut armoire, when eager purchasers began accosting Gail, checkbooks in hand.

Within ten minutes, she sold a washstand, a pie safe, and the armoire. Giddy with elation, she thought: This is heady stuff!

She dashed into the crowded barn, grasped the end of a pine trestle table and, putting her back to it, pulled it along after her. All at once she felt firm hands grip the other end and slam the legs down on the barn floor, holding it fast. She whirled around.

"Tyler!" she shrieked, aghast. "You should have stayed in bed!"

Red-faced, fiery-eyed, he stood leaning on the far end of the table, palms spread flat on the top, holding it down. Accusingly, he said, "I thought you were selling old clothes, stuff we don't want."

"I am!" Gail snapped.

"You are not selling this table," Tyler said in a cold, barely controlled tone.

"I *am* selling it, Tyler!"

"You are *not!* I've spent a year of Sundays refinishing it, and I'm not going to see it snatched away from here."

"But you've never finished refinishing it," Gail said reasonably. "We've never used it. Never will. Someone may as well enjoy it. Besides, I found it in the first place."

Tyler set his jaw and hung onto the table, refusing to budge. Eyes locked, they stood glaring at each other across the long mellow pine no-man's-land between them.

Gail's angry gaze fixed on Tyler's gray hooded sweat shirt. "Did you have to wear that sweat shirt?"

Tyler looked down at his gray-clad chest. "What's wrong with this sweat shirt?"

She glared at the inscription emblazoned on his chest. "I don't think CAVEAT EMPTOR encourages people to buy."

"On the contrary," Tyler replied coolly. "'Let the buyer beware' lets everyone know we're honest or we wouldn't dare warn them to beware."

"I think it tells them to watch out or we'll rook them. So please take it off!"

The next moment a short, round, blond-haired woman in a patchwork rabbit fur jacket and beret bustled up to Gail and thrust some bills in her hand.

"I'll take that darling old Lincoln rocker sitting out by the lamppost."

"Lincoln rocker!" Tyler roared. "Gail, you didn't put my Lincoln rocker on the block!"

In tones of infinite patience, Gail said softly, "Tyler, you can't take it with you to Tahiti, or to heaven, or to..."

"Listen, Gail! It's *my* rocker, and it's not for sale!" He snatched the bills from Gail's hand, flipped open the would-be customer's shoulder bag, and stuffed the money inside.

"Well, I never!" snapped the woman, gazing at Gail reproachfully. "You'd think a person would know what she has to sell before she put an ad in the paper!" In high dudgeon, she waddled out of the barn like an angry duck.

Gail wheeled on Tyler. "You mustn't snarl at people like that. You'll drive them all away! You just can't..."

Swiftly, Tyler sidestepped around her and streaked outside. She hurried out after him and saw him fling himself down in his Lincoln rocker. He gripped the arms with both hands, as if defending his citadel against all comers. His eyes shone with a fiercely protective gleam that called to Gail's mind a golden eagle guarding his nest. She smiled to herself, thinking: Tyler, too, is a rare bird, definitely an endangered species.

Shy among the throng of people milling around, Gail

made her way into the former tack room. She inhaled deeply, enjoying the lingering smells of old leather and saddle soap and Neat's foot oil. She lighted a fire in a black, pot-bellied stove and put a pot of coffee on to boil. She rang up her money and checks on the antique brass cash register she'd set up on a card table, then poured herself a mug of steaming coffee and sank down on a dilapidated daybed. She was sipping the fragrant coffee, warming her hands on the mug, when she heard excited shouts, sounds of a commotion outside.

She leaped to her feet and raced outside to the turnaround. A crowd of spectators had gathered around the Queen Anne highboy. To her horror, she saw Tyler clinging to it for dear life, his arms stretched around it, hugging it like a lover embracing his mistress.

As she raced toward him, someone shouted, "Here she is now!" A huge, granite-faced man stepped from the circle of onlookers. In harsh tones he said, "That sign posted there on the barn door says you have a four-poster for sale, but your husband won't let me see it. He says it's not for sale!"

A thin, reedy, sharp-eyed, sharp-nosed woman chimed in, "And I'm innarested in this here Queen Anne, and now he says that ain't for sale neither! Are you havin' a sale here today, lady, or ain't you?"

Gail glowered at Tyler, murder in her eyes. "That is *my* Queen Anne highboy, and it *is* for sale, and so is the four-poster bed."

"They are *not* for sale!" Tyler thundered. "Woman, would you sell the very bed out from under your loving husband?"

A burst of laughter rippled through the crowd. Gail's cheeks burned with humiliation and rage. "How can you sell a bed out from under a husband who refuses to lie in it!" she blurted out. "Besides, I found the bed *and* the highboy. Both are for sale!"

"Wrong!" Tyler yelled. He turned to the irate man and woman and placing a hand on each of their shoulders, said in friendly, placating tones, "Now, I'll tell you what I'm going to do—just for you—because I want to make things right, and my wife certainly misled you, misrepresented the sale items..."

Sudden fury overrode shyness. Gail shrieked, "That isn't true! Don't listen to him! Just look at him!" She thrust a deprecatory finger under Tyler's nose. "Would you buy a used car from that man?"

As if she hadn't spoken, Tyler went on in smooth, flowing tones, mesmerizing his audience. "The truth is, that old Queen Anne is on her last legs."

Gail let out a strangled cry. "Of course she's on her last legs! Her last legs are her first legs! She's an original, in mint condition!" Her voice faded, her courage failed. Tyler continued his silver-tongued speech.

"And that old four-poster, that's seen a heap of wear, I can tell you!" Another ripple of laughter fluttered through the crowd. "Now, if the little lady of the house doesn't have it out here where you can see it in the clear light of day, well, I don't need to tell you there has got to be a reason—something's mighty wrong with that bed!"

Furious at Tyler, Gail wanted to shout, "Don't listen to him! He's the last of the Yankee peddlers! He could sell vacuum cleaners to desert tribesmen!" But the words stuck in her throat.

"Now, I'll tell you what I'm going to do. I'm going to find the best Queen Anne highboy and the finest four-poster in all of New England just for you. And I'm going to give them to you at the dealer's price, taking no profit for myself. I want to make it up to you for all the trouble

you've been through at the hands of the little lady here."
He shot Gail a scathing glance. "Now, you just give me
your names and phone numbers and I'll be calling you
next week."

Reassured, heads nodded and smiles broadened on the
stern faces in the crowd. A few skeptics, who apparently
doubted that Gail was selling anything worthwhile, left.
New customers came and went throughout the day. Tyler,
in a perpetual frenzy, continued to accost them, insisting
his favorite antiques were not for sale.

Driven to distraction, Gail tried to stop him, all in
vain. The trouble was, most of the time she couldn't
remember whose side of the family which antiques came
from, so when Tyler indignantly claimed them as his
own, she hadn't a leg to stand on. To make matters
worse, he absolutely refused to change his CAVEAT EMP-
TOR sweat shirt.

When the sun sank over the yardarm and the last car
had rolled down the lane, Gail stomped inside the house
and slammed the door after her.

Tyler flung open the door, stomped inside the house,
and slammed the door after him. "What are you so steamed
about?"

"Tyler Phineas Peabody, I'm so mad at you, I could—
could cut off your food! For years, I've been waiting for
my ship to come in. Now, just as it's sailing into port,
you're trying to scuttle it. How dare you tell people things
aren't for sale when they are. I found that bed and the
Queen Anne, myself, and I have every right to sell them!"

"Ha!" Tyler said, stripping off his gloves and throwing
them down on the table. "I'm the one who should be
mad. I spent two of the best years of my life refinishing
that Queen Anne. But never mind, darling. I see what
you're doing. You're trying to coerce me to make me

change my mind about leaving. Well, it won't work."

"Ha!" Gail hooted. "I wouldn't keep you here against your will for the world! Why don't you just take off now instead of staying on till the fourteenth? I'll hold my next sale without you and I'll probably do much, *much* better!"

"Your *next* sale! You've got to be kidding!"

Relentlessly, she shook her head. "I'm holding a sale every Saturday—until everything I want to sell is sold!"

Disbelief flooded Tyler's face. "You wouldn't sell *my* things, my heirlooms, left to me by my grandparents on both sides, and my father and Daphne."

"If there's a buyer..." Gail gave a helpless shrug.

Tyler's expression of disbelief turned to indignation. He flung out his arms in a gesture of outrage. "Before you know it, the house will be empty. You can't live in an empty house. What will you do?"

Coolly, Gail said, "I will rent it and move into a condo, as I explained to you before. Obviously, you were not listening, you were doing your crossword puzzle."

"All right, all right! You can sell *your* heirlooms, but not *mine*. I'm putting all mine in storage and taking off."

Looking shocked and appalled at the same time, Gail sank onto a chair. "Tyler, you wouldn't, couldn't, move your furniture out of this house while I'm still living in it! That's not very gallant!"

Tyler let out a long, deep sigh. "No, I suppose it isn't. But you'll probably sell most of your things at your sale next Saturday." His eyes gleamed with a fiery light. "And don't try to sell any of mine, because I'll be right here, guarding them!"

"I'm glad you mentioned that," Gail said sweetly, "because before you put any of your heirlooms in storage, you'll have to determine which are yours and which are mine."

"No problem," Tyler said affably. "Daphne can tell . . ."

"Daphne is driving all over the U.S. and Canada with the marvelous atlas you gave her!"

Tyler looked as if she'd shot him with an arrow. Gail felt a small stab of pleasure. For the first time in living memory, Tyler Phineas Peabody was speechless.

During the week that followed, when Tyler was not shopping for his trip, or repacking in a more efficient way, he was out in the station wagon scouring farm sales and flea markets, searching the hills and valleys for the highboy and four-poster he had promised the irate buyer and her friend.

On Tuesday morning, Tyler found the four-poster, but not one highboy, let alone a Queen Anne. Each day he drove farther afield. On Friday he came home in a jubilant mood bearing a butcher's block and a brass cash register. "John McCall, down the road a piece, said he was looking for a butcher's block," Tyler explained sheepishly. "And Sally Williams tried to buy our cash register. So I just picked these up for John and Sally."

Gail nodded her approval. "That was a nice, neighborly thing to do, Tyler. I've stashed some things in the barn to sell next Saturday. You'd better look them over—make sure I'm not selling anything you want to hang on to."

"You bet I will!" He stomped outside to the barn.

Gail joined Tyler a few minutes later, to find him bristling with indignation, one hand placed possessively on the top of a rolltop desk.

"I can't believe you'd sell this desk! It's unique, a treasure, not to mention the fact that it was handed down to us by my side of the family."

"What do you mean, *your* side of the family!" Gail

said indignantly. "That desk has belonged to my uncle Nathaniel ever since I can remember."

"You have a short memory, darling. That desk has been in my family for two hundred years!"

"Your memory is much longer than you realize, my love, because the desk is only one hundred ten years old." Swiftly, she rolled back the top, pulled open a drawer, and withdrew a paper, yellowed and stiff with age. Wordlessly, she handed it to Tyler. It was a bill of sale dated April 8, 1874, marked: "Paid by Nathaniel Wilson."

Tyler had the grace to blush. "Well, sometimes I get carried away."

"I understand, my love," Gail said warmly. "And if the desk means that much to you, I won't sell it. I'll let you put it in storage with your other heirlooms."

"Storage!" Tyler exclaimed, staring at her as if she'd lost her mind. "You know damned well storage is death to a rolltop. It should be in someone's home—in *your* home."

"I'd love to keep it for you," Gail said, sounding genuinely sorry, "but there won't be room enough in my condo." At his crestfallen expression, she averted her gaze, afraid she might weaken. She picked up a pen and the yellow sale tag from the desk, scratched out the price, and wrote SOLD.

On the following Saturday, Gail and Tyler were prepared for people driving up their lane, as Tyler put it, at the crack of dawn, and pounding on their door. This time, to Gail's great relief, he took the sale in good grace and went out with her to open up the barn and help haul the antiques they had agreed to sell outside to the turnaround. And this time, believing in being prepared, she had hidden Tyler's CAVEAT EMPTOR sweat shirt in the bottom of the laundry basket.

Gail watched Tyler from the corner of her eye. He seemed to enjoy talking with the customers, telling them the family history of a Tiffany lamp, or a shaving stand. And if he didn't know the history, he invented one. Privately, she took him to task for dissembling. His russet brows rose in astonished innocence. Vehemently, he denied that he had deceived anyone. He had not exaggerated the worth of any item, and, besides, he insisted, buyers loved to be told a story. He was merely being accommodating.

Gail gazed at him in admiration. "Tyler, you are the only person I know who can think faster than sound!"

Late in the afternoon Gail heard a tall, distinguished-looking gray-haired woman asking Tyler if he had a hall tree stashed away in the barn or attic.

Tyler rubbed his chin in thoughtful concentration. "No, but I spotted one at Old Forge Antiques last week. Tell you what. I'm driving up there tomorrow to see about a highboy. If the hall tree's still there, I'll pick it up for you."

Another customer, overhearing the conversation, pounced on Tyler. "Would you mind awfully looking for a Jenny Lind bed for my daughter? She wants one so badly..."

His face broke out in a magnanimous smile. "Sure thing. Be glad to hunt one up for you. No trouble at all." He took a scrap of paper and a stub of a pencil from his jacket pocket. "Tell me your name and phone number."

Smiling to herself, Gail shook her head. Tyler was a born wheeler-dealer. Then, with the suddenness of a thunderclap in a summer storm, an idea struck her. Perhaps she could postpone Tyler's Great Escape a little longer . . .

On Sunday Tyler took off in the station wagon to find the items he'd promised. He returned exuding a mixture of disappointment and pleasure. Old Forge Antiques had not located the highboy, as Tyler had hoped, but he had found both the hall tree and the Jenny Lind bed. Gail went with him out to the barn to look them over.

She ran her fingertips over the satin-smooth knobs on the headboard, admired the grain of the walnut hall tree. "They're lovely, Tyler. And it's great that you found them, but we haven't carved a path through our own things. The attic is still bulging at the rafters." Relentlessly, she went on: "I'm afraid I'll have to hold another sale, and you'll just have to trust me not to sell your things."

She was gratified to see an uneasy frown darken Tyler's face. She stepped onto the platform of an old white wooden garden swing and sank down on the seat. With one toe, she touched the seat facing hers and set the swing swaying to and fro. "And I don't know what to tell that woman whom you promised the highboy. You did promise her, and you are a man of your word— aren't you?"

Tyler suddenly looked like a man nailed to the wall. His distraught gaze locked with her impassive one. He stepped onto the swing and sat down across from her. He let out a deep sigh, heavy with the weight of responsibility. "Well, I've put off going this long—I guess I can put it off one more week. It will give me time to track down the highboy, and give you time to sell the rest of your things."

"Oh, I don't know if I can sell everything next Saturday, Tyler. It may take two Saturdays, or three or more.

Of course, it would go much faster if you were here to help."

She could almost hear the wheels going around in Tyler's head. He was probably thinking he owed it to her to help her out, and that he could keep an eye on which things were sold, make sure his own were safe.

Tyler gave a reluctant nod. "I guess I'll stay till we've sold all the stuff we want to sell and I put mine in storage. But I'm still worried about the rolltop."

Feeling a sudden wave of sympathy for him, Gail said in conciliatory tones, "Even though it's my uncle Nathaniel's desk, I'll give it to you, since you're losing Sidney."

Tyler brightened. "That's decent of you, love. And maybe Daphne will adopt the rolltop."

Gail grinned. "Along with J. Alfred Prufrock. I'll rent a trailer and drive them down to her when she gets home."

Relief flooded Tyler's ruddy features. "Then it's up, up, and away, for me!"

"Right on, Tyler. Upward and onward!" Gail's lips curved in an enigmatic smile.

For a long moment, Tyler stared at her in thoughtful, contemplative silence. At last he said softly, "When you smile like that, that little Mona Lisa smile that just curls the corners of your mouth, it makes me nervous."

"Oh, why so, Tyler?"

He cocked his head, as if considering. "Well, it makes me feel that you know a secret you're not telling me."

Gail's smile widened. "That's right, Tyler. And as you yourself have so often said, that's what makes me so fascinating, so mysterious, and so intriguing." Still smiling, she leaned forward and kissed him full on the lips. Once again, Tyler forgot to deny himself. And Gail forgot to remind him.

 12

THE NEWS PASSED swiftly by word of mouth throughout
the village and beyond that the Peabodys were selling
out; that they had more antiques than they had counted;
and whatever people wanted that they didn't have, Tyler
Peabody would find for them.

The following Saturday, rather than the crowd thin-
ning out, more and more customers came flocking to
their barn. Gail began to get into the swing of things.
With airy confidence, she told a buyer that of course
Tyler would refinish the top of a piecrust table to get rid
of that nasty cigarette burn. Glancing at Tyler, she saw
his eyes bug out. He gave a vigorous shake of his head.
Quickly, she turned away. It wasn't until she promised
someone he would refinish a Winthrop desk that he rebelled outright.

"I don't have time, Gail. This week I promised to
find a player piano for the woman who bought the Jenny
Lind bed. And I may have to run down to Boston—Joe
Conners at the Old Forge thinks he's tracked down a

Queen Anne highboy for me..."

Gravely, Gail nodded. "I understand, Tyler. I won't promise that you'll refinish any more pieces—but you will refinish the desk, won't you? I've already promised."

Tyler sighed. "I'll try, my love. I'll try."

On the weekend of the third Saturday sale, Tyler stood in the turnaround, his arm around Gail's shoulders, watching the last of the treasure seekers drive away down the lane.

"We sold a helluva lot of stuff today."

"Right. And I got my price on the Tiffany lamp."

"I thought you'd already sold that lamp."

"Uh, I did. This is another one."

"I didn't know we had two Tiffany lamps."

"We sold yours the first week. This one was mine."

"You know another thing we got a terrific price on?" Tyler said happily. "That set of Haviland china."

"The one on the library table in the back of the barn?"

"Right. That lady fell on it like she'd struck gold, hidden back there in the corner. I was as surprised as she was. I didn't remember that we had any Haviland."

"Well, you can't expect to remember everything, Tyler."

"I know, but you'd think I'd remember a set of Haviland china."

"No, I wouldn't, Tyler," Gail insisted a little too vehemently. At once her tone turned soft and consoling. "Don't try to remember everything. It will only upset you. Forgetting is a sign of age. You have to expect to forget things, because, after all, you *are* getting older."

Tyler sighed. "Isn't everyone?"

"Almost. And the alternative isn't very appealing."

Tyler made a habit of taking off every Monday morning in the station wagon to make his rounds of yard sales and auctions and flea markets. If he didn't find what he was looking for, he went out the next morning and the next. Every afternoon he would put on his old faded jeans and his gray CAVEAT EMPTOR sweat shirt and hurry out to the barn. He would spend the afternoon in the tack room warmed by the pot-bellied stove, whistling happily to himself while he treated nicks, scratches, and dents on tabletops, chests, and chair seats.

Shortly before noon on the Monday before her fourth Saturday sale, Gail, who had been out in the VW all morning, drove into the barn. It was cold and blustery outside, and she decided to wait till later to unload her purchases. With a mixture of surprise and relief, she saw that the station wagon was gone. A stroke of fortune. She could unload everything now. Humming a little tune, she jumped out of the car, turned the key in the lock, and threw up the hood. She was bending down, reaching inside, when a voice behind her said, "Need some help, love?"

Gail started guiltily. A choked scream rising in her throat died, stillborn. Swiftly, she straightened, slammed down the hood, and whirled around. "Tyler. What are you doing home?"

Tyler grinned. "Sorry I scared you. But why shouldn't I be home?"

Gail fumbled for words. "Well, no reason, except that you don't normally get home till much later on Mondays. And the wagon's gone. I thought *you* were gone."

"I left it at the service station in the village to have the oil changed," Tyler said amiably. "Charlie ran me home. Maybe you can drive me over in the morning to pick it up."

"Oh, sure, Tyler." She reached toward the keys in the

lock. "Well, I'm going in to start dinner."

"Don't you want to unload the food first?"

"There's nothing in there for dinner. I'll do it later."

"We'd better unload now, while I'm here to help you."
He flung up the hood, took one look, then jerked backward, erupting in a thunderous shout. "Good Lord in heaven!"

Gail smiled and gave a nonchalant wave of her hand.
"I, I—uh, picked up a few things while I was out."

Tyler seemed at a loss for words. At last he nodded, as if glimpsing a ray of light at the end of a tunnel. "You picked up another Tiffany lamp, an inlaid mahogany writing box, three pairs of silver candlesticks, two brass doorknockers"—he leaned forward and peered into a cardboard box—"and a few pieces of Canton china." His mouth quirked at the corners. "It's wonderful what you can buy at the supermarket these days."

She thought she detected a knowing gleam in his eyes, as though he was putting her on. "I didn't say I got them at the supermarket," she said huffily.

"Where *did* you get them?"

She tossed her hair back over her shoulder in an independent gesture. "Oh, out and about—farm sales, auctions."

"The same place you got the other Tiffany lamp, and the Haviland china and the Willow ware platter and piano stool?"

Her head snapped back. She gazed up at him in stunned stupefaction. Tyler burst out laughing.

"Tyler, you knew!" she cried. "You knew all the time!"

He chuckled, shaking his head. "Not *all* the time. I began to suspect after the second Tiffany lamp showed up. Then I started watching you. But I never could catch you in the act—till now. How did you manage, any-way?"

A sheepish expression came over her face. "When you took off to buy special pieces for customers, I took off to replenish our stock. I had the big pieces delivered on Monday mornings, when I knew you'd be off on safari. I stashed the small things in the trunk of the car. Then, at night, when I was sure you were sound asleep, I'd get them out of the trunk and hide them away in the attic to gather a little dust."

Tyler placed his big hands gently on her shoulders and gazed intently into her face. The laughter in his eyes faded, replaced by a look of such depth and yearning that it took her breath away. Quietly, he said, "And as fast as we sold off our antiques, you replaced them with others."

Mutely, she nodded. Tyler's image blurred, swam before the sudden mist in her eyes.

He sank down on a pile of hay spilling from one of the bales in the corner and pulled her down beside him.

"Why, Gail?" Tyler asked softly. "Tell me why."

A hushed silence trembled in the air. Then her words tumbled out in a breathless rush. "You said you'd stay till we sold everything we wanted to sell. It was the only way I could think of to keep you here." She swallowed hard, forcing down tears that threatened to choke her. In ragged tones, she went on: "I couldn't let you go away. I love you, Tyler. You know that. But I need you, too, need you like crazy to share my life. I don't want to walk without you, Tyler." Unable to endure the look of shocked understanding, of incredulity, on his face, she buried her head on his shoulder. His arms tightened around her.

"Gail, Gail, my little love," he whispered. "Like the

willow, bending with the wind, going along with whatever life hands out, never giving up. Storms may rage around you, but when they're over, there you stand, undaunted, undefeated..." He paused, kissing her forehead, her eyelids, the tip of her nose, her lips.

"You've always done such a good job of rolling with the punches, love, that I thought all you needed in life was your sculpture. You've never needed people clustering around you, and after I was promoted to company headquarters and stayed home all the time, it seemed you didn't need me." He smiled wryly. "I thought all you needed was a bronze bust—that you'd be completely happy without me."

Gail raised her head from his shoulder, lifting her tear-streaked face to his. "But, Tyler. I told you my sculpting means nothing without you."

Tyler gave a rueful smile. "Loyalty is one of your many fine traits, my love. I thought you were being loyal."

"Me, a martyr!" Gail cried, feigning outrage.

He kissed her again. "You must admit, darling, you did tell me more than once that you wouldn't dream of keeping me against my will...to go, and Godspeed!"

Gail frowned. "I wouldn't want a man who didn't want me, a man who stayed with me against his will."

A shadow of pain crossed his face. Solemnly, he went on: "But don't you see? You were the one who went away. You shut me out of your life."

"Oh, Tyler, no!" Gail cried. "I never meant to. I was only trying to make a life for myself, to keep out of your way while you were climbing your corporate ladder."

Tyler rested his chin on her head and stroked her long, glossy hair. "That never occurred to me, my love, because I thought I knew you, because we've always thought alike, ever since the day we met." He clasped her shoulders and held her away from him, studying her face. A reflective look came into his clear, light brown eyes.

"I thought we still thought alike," Gail murmured in choked tones. "What happened to us, Tyler?"

"We were both so involved doing our own thing that we never had time for each other, never made time to talk. As the years flew past, we took different turnings. And each of us was unaware of the twists and turns the other's thoughts were taking."

Numbly, Gail nodded. "I thought what you wanted was to be at the top of the corporate heap at Liberty Life."

Tyler sighed deeply. "I thought so, too. I did want it. And I've had it. Now I'm ready to move on."

"Like running off to Tahiti," Gail said wistfully. "Well, you're free to go." Looking chagrined, she went on: "You've found me out, discovered my game to keep you here, caught me in my own web."

"Just how long did you think you could keep on buying antiques to replace what we sold, darling?"

Gail shrugged. A mischievous light sprang to her eyes. "Scheherazade told stories for a thousand and one nights."

Tyler crooked a finger under her chin, raising her face to his. He grinned down at her. "And you were aiming for a thousand and one Saturdays!"

Gail stared intently into his eyes. A small, secret smile quirked the corners of her mouth. "Tyler, that's not a bad idea. Not bad at all. Why couldn't we keep on buying and selling antiques for a thousand and one Saturdays? You love chatting with the customers, telling tall tales and short tales about every stick of furniture. You'd be your own boss . . ."

"And there would be no terrible train ride to and fro,

no regimentation, no schedules or deadlines!" A spark of enthusiasm kindled and grew in Tyler's eyes. Gail's hopes soared. The longer they talked, the better it sounded.

Tyler threw an arm about her shoulders and gave her an affectionate hug. "You know what I've discovered now that we've finally gotten around to talking things out?"

"Tell me, quick!"

"Each of us brings something unique to our marriage, so that together we make a team greater than each of us could be alone."

Gail gave a vehement nod. "Oh, that's so true, Tyler. Who said that?"

"I did." He gazed thoughtfully at a cobweb in a corner of the doorway, glistening in the late-afternoon sunlight. "Actually, I imprisoned myself. I admit I was enchanted with the fantasy of the Great Escape. But if we went into the antiques business, I'd be free to be my own person, to do my own thing."

Gail regarded him lovingly. Her lips brushed his. "And you wouldn't be restless and discontent?"

"Not with you here, my love. You've come back to me, right? You're no longer shutting me out for clay and plaster. Right?"

Gail nodded vigorously.

His tone turned sober, his face grave. "You see, Gail, I've discovered that I need you as much as you need me."

Gail shook her head. "You could have fooled me! You were so eager to fly off to Tahiti without me, I didn't think you cared."

His arms tightened around her. "I care," Tyler said fervently. "I should have told you more often. I care more about you than you'll ever know. You are my whole life, now and forever. And in the days and months and years to come, we'll have time for each other—starting now!" He lay back on the pile of hay and pulled her close to his side.

In a matter of moments, Gail's fur-trimmed parka and Tyler's gray sweat shirt were spread beneath them. In their joy at finding one another again, they kissed hungrily, touching, fondling, caressing, warmed by the heat of their passion. They embraced eagerly, letting go all the pent-up desire that had been dammed behind a high, thick wall of misunderstanding. Tyler had never been so ardent, so adventuresome in his lovemaking, awakening in Gail new depths of feeling. She responded eagerly, fully, with an ardor she hadn't known she possessed.

He knelt over her, straddling her hips. His warm, sensitive fingers explored flesh and bone, finding secret places, undiscovered shores. An ecstatic cry of delight escaped her. "Oh, Tyler," she said tremulously, "if this is what your newfound freedom does to you, let's be forever free!" The rest of their clothes joined the sweat shirt and parka.

Steeped in a delicious languor, Gail heard Tyler murmur huskily all the loving words she longed to hear. Through half-closed lids, in a shaft of sunlight sifting through the doorway, she saw his body bent over hers, and his face was radiant with love. Fiery lights glinted in his russet hair. Beads of sweat gleamed on his shoulders, his brow. The stringent scent of his body heat mingled with the smell of sweet, dry, musty hay and the woodsmoke from the pot-bellied stove.

Fiercely, she gripped his shoulders and pulled him close, holding him tightly to her, crushing her breasts against his warm, hairy chest. She heard his swift intake of breath, felt his muscles bunch as if gathering in, then the powerful thrust of his body against hers. An exquisite burst of pleasure akin to pain exploded inside her, traveling in tiny wavelets to the tip of every nerve ending, stirring the very core of her soul.

After some little time, when they had slaked their thirst for one another and lay drifting and dreaming in each other's arms, Gail said softly, "Tyler, I may never finish your bust. You are much more desirable and responsive than clay and plaster—even a bronze bust can never do justice to the real you."

"I agree one hundred ten percent, darling." He gave her bottom a friendly pinch. "There's nothing like the real thing." A devilish glint glistened in his eyes. "I think we've found the real me."

She captured his strong hands in her slender fingers. "Don't try to sidetrack me, Tyler." She looked up at him, love, faith, and trust shining in her eyes. "Then you'll cancel every last ticket, every last reservation, with marvelous Miss Curtis?"

Tyler nuzzled her ear. "Promise."

During the days that followed, Gail was deliriously happy—until late one Friday afternoon when she and Sidney brought in the mail. Sorting through letters, bills, and ads, she found a thick letter addressed to Tyler from the travel agency. She felt as if she were turning to stone. Frantically, she ran her fingers over the envelope, feeling what was inside . . . something with stiff backing, like an airline ticket. Tears welled in her eyes. Sidney flew to her side. "Sidney," she burst out, "I can't believe this is happening!"

She ran to the window and held the envelope up to the light. Yes, there was definitely a ticket inside! She felt unutterably crushed, betrayed. Her first impulse was to toss the letter into the fire. With a great effort of will, she fought it down. Sternly, she told herself there must be some mistake. Miss Curtis simply did not understand that Tyler had canceled his plans. She would call that female Pied Piper herself and tell her what was what! She started toward the phone and immediately thought better of it. The news would be better coming from Tyler. But Tyler was gone, hunting for a captain's chair. She set her lips in a grim line, scarcely able to contain her wrath until he came home. She started dinner, slamming pots and pans around as if there would be no tomorrow.

Half an hour later Tyler strode into the keeping room, exuding good-natured cheer. "Well, I found the captain's chair! What's new with you?"

Gail took a deep breath to keep her composure and riveted him with a direct, unblinking gaze. Snatching up the envelope, she thrust it into his hands. "This!"

He glanced down at it. His lips split in a jubilant smile. "They've come!" he said happily.

"What's come?" Gail demanded.

"My tickets," Tyler said, as calmly and unconcerned as if he'd never promised to cancel his plans with Miss Curtis.

Any second, Gail thought, I am going to fly into a million pieces. She swept up a cast-iron mallet and began to pound a Swiss steak to within an inch of its life.

With a flourish, Tyler placed the envelope in the center of the table. "This calls for a celebration. It's a festive occasion, my love!" With no further explanation, he lighted the candles on the table and poured them each a glass of rich, red Cabernet Sauvignon.

"Come and sit down, Gail. I want to propose a toast."

"The steak isn't done." She turned her back to him and tossed a green salad, giving off a dark, ominous silence like a thundercloud about to burst.

As if unaware of her dark mood, Tyler's eyes glowed with pleasure. "Never mind. This is more important!"

Gail slid into her chair. Savagely, she thought: Must he be so devastatingly cheerful? White-lipped, in tight, choked tones, she said, "I thought you were going to cancel your reservations, tell Miss Curtis you didn't want those tickets!"

Tyler's brows rose with injured innocence. "Oh, I did, I did." He nodded at the letter. "Open it!"

Gail ripped open the envelope. A burning ache seared her heart. She found exactly what she expected to find—an airline-ticket folder. Quietly, she handed it to Tyler. In dull, defeated tones she said, "I get the message, Tyler. You're still going to go on your trip."

Tyler nodded. "Open the folder."

Numbly, with stiff fingers, she withdrew the ticket, saw Tyler's name. She started to put it down.

"Hang in there," Tyler said, smiling. "There's a surprise."

Gail stared at him wordlessly, unable to go on. She had already guessed his surprise. He had bought a return ticket as well. He was doing her a big favor: letting her know not only that he would definitely return, but when!

Eagerly, Tyler lunged across the table, swept the tickets from her hands, shuffled through them, and slapped one on top.

"There, feast your eyes on that!"

She stared at him in disbelief. How could he be so insensitive, so downright cruel?

"Go on," he urged, smiling. "Read it."

She glanced down at the ticket, then glanced up at Tyler, and glanced down again, frowning. It looked exactly the same as it had before, except for one letter.

"Tyler!" she shrieked. "There's an 's' after the letters 'Mr'!"

"You got it!" Tyler shouted. "The winning ticket, darling, for Mrs. Tyler Peabody."

After a long, dumbfounded moment, Gail burst out, "Oh, Tyler, you sweet thing. But—but I thought you wanted to go by yourself?"

Grinning, Tyler said, "I've concluded that man cannot live on breadfruit alone. You, my love, are the woman I'd most like to be stranded on a desert island with. A marriage should be two who walk together on the same path, not one leading and the other walking three steps behind. We'll walk together on the Road of Loving Hearts. We'll stay in Tahiti until we tire of living like Rousseau's children of nature."

Gail gave him a radiant smile. "And then we'll come home and sell antiques for one thousand and one Saturdays."

Tyler raised his glass in salute. "One thousand and one—and more!"

Smiling happily, Gail touched her glass to his. "And more," she said softly. "Together—down the Road of Loving Hearts."

WONDERFUL ROMANCE NEWS!

Do you know about the exciting SECOND CHANCE AT LOVE/TO HAVE AND TO HOLD newsletter? Are you on our *free* mailing list? If reading all about your favorite authors, getting sneak previews of their latest releases, and being filled in on all the latest happenings and events in the romance world sound good to you, then you'll love our SECOND CHANCE AT LOVE and TO HAVE AND TO HOLD Romance News.

If you'd like to be added to our mailing list, just fill out the coupon below and send it in…and we'll send you your *free* newsletter every three months — hot off the press.

☐ *Yes, I would like to receive your free SECOND CHANCE AT LOVE/TO HAVE AND TO HOLD newsletter.*

Name _____

Address _____

City _____ State/Zip _____

Please return this coupon to:

Berkley Publishing
200 Madison Avenue, New York, New York 10016
Att: Rebecca Kaufman

HERE'S WHAT READERS ARE SAYING ABOUT

To Have and to Hold™

"Your TO HAVE AND TO HOLD series is a fabulous and long overdue idea."
— *A. D., Upper Darby, PA**

"I have been reading romance novels for over ten years and feel the TO HAVE AND TO HOLD series is the best I have read. It's exciting, sensitive, refreshing, well written. Many thanks for a series of books I can relate to."
— *O. K., Bensalem, PA**

"I enjoy your books tremendously."
— *J. C., Houston, TX**

"I love the books and read them over and over."
— *E. K., Warren, MI**

"You have another winner with the new TO HAVE AND TO HOLD series."
— *R. P., Lincoln Park, MI**

"I love the new series TO HAVE AND TO HOLD."
— *M. L., Cleveland, OH**

"I've never written a fan letter before, but TO HAVE AND TO HOLD is fantastic."
— *E. S., Narberth, PA**

*Name and address available upon request

Second Chance at Love®